T0132491

AuthorHouse™
1663 Liberty Drive
Bloomington, IN 47403
www.authorhouse.com
Phone: 1 (800) 839-8640

Published by AuthorHouse 07/26/2018

ISBN: 978-1-5462-5285-6 (sc)
ISBN: 978-1-5462-5284-9 (e)

Library of Congress Control Number: 2018908742

Print information available on the last page.

Murder stalks the halls of Meadowdale Manor, a retirement community in Garland, Texas. Laurel Baley and Olive Harting, whose husbands are in the Memory Care Unit, suspect a bit of larceny and mismanagement are afoot, and join forces to uncover the villains. Soon they are joined by other "guests" of Meadowdale and mayhem ensues.

CHAPTER 1

It was a very small Faberge egg, hardly noticeable as it sat in the busy shadow box above the television set. But its absence was very noticeable to Sophie Feldstein. It had been a gift from her children for their fiftieth wedding anniversary.

She and Mortimer Feldstein had enjoyed fifty-two years together before he passed. That was when her children selected Meadowdale Manor for their mother. Of course it was guilt that drove them to make sure she was close enough to visit each week. And now it was guilt that caused Sophie to question whether to report the egg missing.

What if she had moved it while dusting? Or had put it away for safe keeping? At seventy-four she was too young to be losing her mind. But, it was missing.

That evening at dinner, she asked her table-mate Myrtle, if she had heard of anyone else losing things from their Independent Living apartments.

"Well, George complained that his coin collection was missing two Liberty Walking silver dollars. I just figured the old coot spent them," Myrtle said, pushing her thick glasses back up on her nose. "But then, that Mrs. Pho said her antique vase was gone. She suspected an aide had broken it and hid the pieces."

"I never let anyone in my apartment but my children. Oh, and that nice Dr. Patel two weeks ago when I had a nasty cough. He is so attentive." Sophie smiled at the memory of Dr. Patel's visit. His bedside manner was just what she needed.

Sophie lowered her voice. "Should I go to the administration and report it? I wouldn't want them to think I need to go to the second floor."

Myrtle laughed. "You will not be heading for the Memory Unit any time soon, Sophie. When George reported his silver missing, they had him fill out a report, but nothing came of it. Are you sure it is gone?"

"That's just it. I don't know when it went missing," Sophie admitted. "Oye vey, it may turn up again, God willing. Let's go to Bingo tomorrow. Maybe I will get some new hand cream."

At that Myrtle laughed again. The prizes were never that nice.

On the second floor, in the men's Memory Care unit, Olive and Walter were trying to enjoy their dinner.

Olive Harting lifted the glutinous mess carefully with her fork and grimaced. She looked over at her husband, Walter. "Looks good honey. Eat up!" she encouraged him with an overly cheerful voice.

Walter laughed. "I may have lost my mind, but I'm not stupid. It doesn't look very good, does it Olive? If I eat the mac and cheese, can I have some ice cream?" He looked up at her with puppydog eyes and grinned.

"Hmph," she said sternly, then gave him an affectionate

smile. "Okay. But you have to eat it all." Olive fingered her pearl earrings, just to make sure she had put them on that morning. She never felt dressed without her earrings.

He began to spoon the three little mounds of yellow gloop rapidly into his mouth, a bit of cheese oozing from the corner of his lips. Olive was disgusted. The food was only passable, the rooms on Windom Hall were small, and the amenities were almost non-existent.

Olive sighed. At almost $4,700 a month to reside as a "guest" in the Memory Care Unit a person had a choice of trying to keep her loved one comfortable, or hoping he left this life before he lost his humanity.

Olive remembered driving up to Meadowdale Manor to see if this was the best place for Walter. What she saw was an elegant three story building with soaring glass windows, a lovely two story portico, magnificent carved wood doors, and an entrance that was enticing, warm and welcoming.

That was, as long as you stayed on the main floor.

When she went to the second floor, which housed those with various levels of dementia, it all changed. Apparently the decorator had decided those men didn't care about their surroundings. And the administration didn't seem to care what they wore, or what they ate.

Windom Hall and Haliburton were the units for the men, with larger units, Duncan and Williams Halls for the ladies. The men's halls were above the main building. The ladies were on the second floor over the large Independent Living wing of Meadowdale.

Dinner done, Olive walked Walter back to Room 215 which they shared. Walter smiled and winked at the aide who was assisting Calvin (who always wore the grey bathrobe), from the patio to his room.

"She likes me," Walter confided in a loud whisper to Olive.

"You think they all like you!" Olive responded, pulling her tweed jacket closer around herself.

"That's because I am such a sweet guy," he agreed.

Getting Walter settled in his recliner watching "Wheel of Fortune," Olive walked down the pale green corridor to the shadowed alcove where the staff kept the refrigerator stocked with Protein drinks, juice and small ice cream cups.

She got a small cup of vanilla ice cream and a plastic spoon and returned to her room where Laurel was waiting for her.

"These men just don't last," Olive complained to her new best friend, Laurel Baley. "I married a man younger than me for that very reason!"

Laurel laughed. "Well, Martin is older than I am, but I wouldn't trade anything for him."

Olive gave Walter his ice cream, which he began to eat greedily as Olive and Laurel went out to the hall. An aide smiled at the two of them as they passed by, two ladies of such different ages, yet both dressed as professionals in their jackets, soft cotton blouses and slacks.

Together, they went to the east side of the building to locking doors which led to a pretty, enclosed patio. The sun was beginning to set behind them, the clouds were streaked with pink.

Olive quickly punched in the code, and they strolled to the plastic chairs where they could talk in private.

Laurel had left her husband, Martin, sitting in his shared

room watching an old Lash LaRue movie, for the third time that day. Unlike Olive, Laurel could neither afford to retire or reside at Meadowdale Manor with her husband. She still worked as a legal secretary to make ends meet.

Laurel smiled ruefully. "You are the only alert person here 24/7. I appreciate how you keep an eye on everything. Poor Martin's health has really deteriorated in the last few months. If I didn't have to work full time I would try to keep him at home, but it just isn't possible."

"You couldn't do it now, Laurel," Olive said sympathetically. "He needs too much care, too much medication. We sold our home so we could afford to be together here. When I was working as a high school principal we invested in long-term care insurance, but that won't last forever."

"You are telling me!" In anger, Laurel shook her pretty head vigorously, her long brown pony tail switching past her shoulders.

"Barring an emergency, we have enough for Martin to stay less than two years. My salary barely covers my crummy little apartment and living expenses for me!"

Olive responded sympathetically, "I know costs are high for long term care insurance, but costs without it are prohibitive."

"After we sold our home to help pay for Walter's care, I decided it would be easier for me to share a room with Walter. At first they resisted the idea, but Mr. Khan had cut staffing recently, and saw me as being an unpaid assistant."

"When did you decide that Meadowdale was the best choice for Martin?" Olive asked kindly.

Laurel thought for a minute. "Let me tell you about

Martin first. It has been such a change you would never have recognized him a few years ago. He was amazing."

"I don't know if you heard of him. Martin Baley was a sought-after music publisher, and he was wise enough to invest as much as he could, but the two stock market downturns did us in."

"Then, Martin had a severe heart attack four years ago, at age sixty-nine. It was followed by Parkinson's disease which came on with a vengeance. He could barely feed himself, much less handle his daily personal care."

"I have since found out that several of the men here on Windom and Haliburton are Veterans like Martin. He was a Vietnam Vet, so there is a little help from the government."

"The Center for Older Veteran's Rights helped me sign up for something called "Aid in Attendance" which gave us an additional $2,100 a month toward Martin's care."

"It doesn't leave me much after I pay our share. I am a Christian and pray all the time that if he can't live a quality life, that God would take him." Tears began to streak down her face.

"Oh Laurel. I've talked with other caregivers, and this is really a typical response. It isn't just that the money may run out, but these men begin to fade, to become just a shell of themselves. When you love someone, that hurts."

Olive put a comforting arm around her friend. Laurel wiped her eyes quickly and they returned into the hall where aides were picking up trays from the rooms.

As she headed for Martin's room, Calista sashayed by and said sarcastically, "Well, if it ain't Laurel and Harting, the two funniest ladies on the ward. Best get back to Martin, Miss Laurel. The movie is almost over and I **ain't** running it again." She moved off, pulling out her phone to tweet her "funny remarks" to some friend.

"It will be okay," Olive laid her hand reassuring on Laurel's shoulder. "Calista is a pill, but fortunately she is only part time. I like the other aides who work today, but night time is a mess. There is one aid that gets stuck with all the dirty work and both the nurses on the weekend shift take long breaks and never answer a call. They send some little overworked aide and hope there are no problems."

Laurel was glad Olive was there to keep an eye on things, to look out for the men who had no one to visit them.

She walked slowly down the hall back to Martin's room. As Laurel entered Room 211 she pulled the yellow sticky note off the door jam.

"Ends 7:15" it read. She always noted the time the video would finish so the aide could either restart it, or put in another one. It was never a new one. All the videos were in black and white, and either old cowboy movies, comedies or light hearted mysteries.

Martin had regressed after his heart attack. Laurel sighed with resignation. Lovingly she smoothed the wild curls back from his forehead, gently pulled him up from the recliner and helped him settle into his bed.

Martin's roommate, Charles P. Gordon, did not stir. Of course, he rarely stirred. Charles never had visitors, and so spent most of his time in the bed across from Martin, not speaking unless spoken to.

Occasionally he would move to his own forest green Lazyboy recliner, but only to watch the news. He was very fastidious, in his expensive striped green pajamas and doe skin slippers.

Petite and energetic, Bebe Tron was a cheerful aide from the Philippines. Her smile was infectious, especially with the one gold tooth glittering. And Bebe loved to talk. She chattered about Charles, sharing all she gleaned from Nurse Betty.

"Mr. Charles here two years. He rich banker, with big house. No wife, so his sister put him here to keep him safe. That is all I know. But he VERY rich!" Bebe giggled as she said this.

Laurel notice that when a sophisticated thriller like "The Thin Man" or an old Cary Grant movie was playing, Charles positioned himself a bit sideways in the recliner so he could watch without drawing attention to himself.

"Obviously," Laurel had told Olive, "His tastes probably were more like fine wine and Ruth's Chris steak house fare, not cowboy flicks and gummy mac and cheese."

They both laughed at the thought of Charles rooting for Roy Rogers like Martin did, or stealing out in the middle of the night in search of vanilla ice cream like Walter.

Sometimes in the evening when Martin had gone to sleep, Laurel would put in a rollicking comedy like "Arsenic and Old Lace," with Cary Grant and Priscilla Lane and pretend she didn't notice Charles peeping from under his comforter to share her enjoyment of their antics.

Weekdays Laurel could only stay until 9 p.m. Saturday morning and Sunday afternoon she enjoyed visiting with her guy. Early in the day Martin still recognized her and could even carry on some sort of conversation.

In the evening, the Lewy's bodies brought on hallucinations and frustration with his unfamiliar surroundings. Then he asked, "Where is Laurel? When will she come take me home?"

Laurel felt blessed that Martin had a shared room on Windom Hall. These rooms were less expensive, had a smaller dining and visitor area than Haliburton where the rooms for singles were. Windom also had fewer aides.

But it also had Olive. She was someone Laurel could confide in.

CHAPTER 2

Saturday morning when Laurel arrived, she had to wait quite awhile for the elevator. When the doors opened, the elevator was lined with drop cloths and two maintenance men stepped out.

"Can I use the elevator?" asked Laurel.

"Sure," said the bigger man. "We were just moving in a guest to Haliburton."

Laurel first stopped at the nurse's station to sign in, as was required. Then, looking into the small visitor dining area, she noted Olive and Walter were busy with a game of dominoes.

Actually Walter was building roads with them, while Olive was trying to keep them all on the table.

Laurel sat down. "I guess another one is moving over from Julep."

"Not really," Olive told Laurel, "I know you think that priority is given to those who start in Independent Living and run through Julep to get here, but most of the men on Windom and Haliburton are admitted directly, like Walter and Martin."

"Really?" Laurel said in amazement. "I thought that

expensive buy-in for those private apartments would give you an advantage as you aged out as an Indie."

"The longer they can keep them at Julep, the more money they make," Olive confirmed. "I heard one of the nurses explain it to the new aide. It takes fewer aides at Julep. Moving them here is not cost effective. In fact, unless someone dies or moves to LaRonda, on the third floor, they can't come over here."

"But," said Laurel, "is the food any better at Julep or Indie? This food is awful."

"Julep has their own little kitchen because there are only about thirty guests over there. The building is mostly for the rehab unit and the swimming pool. Oh, and there is a big screen theater for Friday and Saturday nights," Olive said. "We aren't allowed there according to our contract."

"That contract," responded Laurel, "said our men were to receive meals according to the physician recommended diets, but I've noticed all the men are served the same thing."

"And I don't understand that," agreed Olive. "I've seen the food for the Indie's. It looked really good. Sometimes they have a salad bar, and the Cinco de Mayo party was a real Mexican spread."

Laurel hugged Olive as she got ready to leave. She went to look in on Martin. He was sleeping peacefully as Gene Autry thwarted another bad guy.

It was getting to be twilight when Martin finally woke up. "When can I go home?" he asked plaintively.

"After dinner," Laurel answered gently. She got him up out of his recliner and they walked to the dining area to join Olive and Walter and two other men.

The dining area only seated eight since most of the

men ate in their rooms. Three aides were scheduled for each meal time to assist on Windom for sixteen men who were suffering from stages of dementia.

Haliburton had two aides for the eight men who had single rooms. That wing had a larger dining room and the Activities Director from Julep came over twice a week to assist with activities.

Olive had heard the names the aides on Haliburton gave their "men."

There was Danny Daytimer, because he was always asking, "What day is this?" or "What are we doing today?"

Harold the Hat had six hats, and he wore a different one each day. Mike Minabird picked up anything loose, and if you tried to take away he would holler, "Mine! Mine!"

Friendly (Chester), would shake hands with everyone and say, "Hello, how are you? I'm Chester. If called by a panther, don't anther." Chester had been an insurance man, and might try to sell you some. Sort of like Peter Pie, "Me oh my, I wish I had some pie." He would say that four or five times a day.

Doc, who actually had been a physician, wore a stethoscope and would talk about hearing the resiticity in the walls. Whatever that meant.

The Turk (Bobby Turkle) was always looking for his home. Bobby was a one-time famous movie producer. No room was safe from his wanderings. No drawer was safe from his rummaging. And, because his family was wealthy, no staff member took anyone's side but his.

Sarge (Carl Sanderson) had been in law enforcement. He was suspicious of everything, sliding down the hall in a secretive manner. Then he might holler, "Hey, hey you there. Stop!" Suddenly an aide would drop everything and hurry over before he tried to handcuff a visitor or another guest on the hall.

Windom Hall had twice the guests, but the aides were good about giving equal treatment. Which meant they were too busy to give preferential treatment.

Laurel stayed for an hour to watch another movie with Martin and then tuck him into bed. After he was settled in, she turned out his bedside lamp and kissed his forehead. He was already asleep.

"Back to my little apartment for another day," Laurel said to herself.

On her way to the elevator she passed Olive and Walter strolling down the hall toward the alcove where the nurses kept the Ensure and other protein drinks.

"He wakes up two or three times in the night and wants his drink," Olive said with a grin. "Guess we will be up awhile. Good night, Laurel."

"Good night Olive," Laurel said, signing out in the book, then pressing the code on the pad by the door. Morning would come early and she needed her sleep. The attorneys at Books and Duhn were deep into a case that was going to trial, and she would be keeping the copy machine hot.

"At least life is peaceful here for the boys," Laurel comforted herself with the thought.

Unfortunately, she was wrong.

CHAPTER 3

When Olive and Walter returned to their room, Bobby Turkle was sitting in Olive's soft brown leather recliner. His shoes were off and he was calmly reading the book that Olive had recently laid down. She sighed.

"Bobby, this is not your room. You belong on Haliburton Hall, remember? Let me help you find your home."

He looked at her with a puzzled expression, as if a stranger had dared to enter his private quarters and he wanted to know why. Olive pushed the intercom by the door. "Calista, please come help Mr. Turkle to Room 202."

Then, knowing it was a tossup whether Calista would bother to come or not, Olive gently assisted Walter into his large brown recliner and opened his drink. "I'll be right back. Look, the Late Show is on," she said with false enthusiasm.

Walter turned his attention to the television as she helped Bobby on with his shoes and led him out the door. Bobby was trouble, but there was nothing that could be done to stop him.

Bobby's former socialite wife, Velma Stein, had lived off his royalties until her third remarriage made her ineligible to receive them. So Velma shipped Bobby off from a nice

Sherman Oaks retirement home to Garland, Texas. Their only daughter, Bobbie Jo, had married an oil man and was settled near Dallas. Her mother named her Roberta Josephine, but she was always Bobbie Jo to her adoring daddy.

It did not help that her husband, Brady Wellston, never could stand the loud-mouthed braggart, and was willing to pay top dollar to keep him away from their home. The staff at Meadowdale Manor got the honor to keeping up with his high jinx and Bobbie Jo only slipped in to see him a few times a month, when she went to get her hair or nails done.

Last week, when Olive had returned with their dinner trays, she noticed her land-line phone was missing. She approached Rani. Olive trusted Rani, a slender aide with her thick black hair always in a tidy braid coiled on the nape of her neck. Rani was studying to be a Registered Nurse, and was very kind and attentive to everyone on the unit.

"Have you seen my phone," Olive asked her. Rani just motioned down the hall, "Mr. Bobby has a phone today, and he has no phone line!"

Olive's sharp eyes had noticed the young P.A., Sanjay Singh, seemed to be on the unit seeing patients more often when Rani was on duty. Her long lashed eyes always dropped demurely when Dr. Singh addressed her directly. Olive could feel the electricity between them.

Olive considered why she had decided to live on the unit with Walter. There was little to do for a mentally sound person. The busy nurses did not have time for conversation with all the paperwork required for charting. The aides, many of whom were foreign born, mostly smiled politely and tried to be of assistance, but did not have the time to sit and chat.

And the men on Windom, most were like Walter, whose conversation might be wise or wild. It could vary within a ten minute interval. Beyond a rollickingly crazy domino game of 42 (the rules were never the same) or sharing a game show on television, Olive had resigned herself to her own company. Growing old was not for sissies.

It did not take her long to notice that there were little things at odds with what should be. "Sometimes I feel like I fell down a rabbit hole, like Alice," Olive had confided to Laurel.

When Olive thought back to how she had chosen Meadowdale Manor, she realized it was like so many other decisions. An ad on television and an internet search had started it all.

Mrs. Brooks, her neighbor, had seen an ad on television, and followed it up with a Web search for memory care units. The top website for Senior Care Housing had popped up, promising four choices "in your area" at whatever level you needed. Olive started referring to it as "PLUM" because they paid a fee for each referral and every facility that contacted her tried to "pick her off."

Mrs. Brooks immediately gave Kimberly of PLUM Olive's home number. Kimberly soon regretted it, because Olive grilled her on every detail, from the cost, the size of the rooms, and what type of care was offered at each facility.

Olive and Walter Harting were both educators, with good retirement incomes and a large nest egg. As a well-educated and self-assured women, Olive was a bit officious as she toured each facility and then badgered each administrator about what was offered and any problems they might have. She was formidable, almost regal, in her tweed suits, sturdy shoes and pearls.

At eighty-two, Olive was determined to make sure Walter (who was two years younger) had the best care possible.

Finally, after two weeks, Olive settled on Meadowdale Manor, where Walter could have the highest level of care in beautiful surroundings. Besides, all the reviews were positive.

Olive Greyn Harting was proud of her Ph.D. in Education. She taught high school twenty-seven years and then retired from being Principle at a small rural high school.

She was determined to read every contract for the minutest detail. She knew Robert's Rules of Order top to bottom. Any committee she was on came to fear her nit picking, although it had saved their bacon in several instances by fending off possible disaster.

Her biggest lament to Laurel was, "nothing really interesting ever happens around here."

Until it did.

CHAPTER 4

Unfortunately, it happened on a Saturday, when the Administrative offices were empty and the only staff was part-timers. Otherwise, the murder would have been solved quickly.

Mykala, much to her distress, had discovered the body in Room 213. His name was James Potter, a very elderly man, who had severe dementia. Potter rarely left his room, and Mykala hurried in about 8:15 to pick up his dinner tray.

It should have been picked up by 7 p.m., but Mykala usually went out for a smoke before making her rounds to pick up trays and help the guests into bed.

As it was, she had run out of cigarettes and drove to a little market a few blocks away to get another pack. While there, she saw a new US magazine, with a story about Jennifer Aniston getting back with Brad. That took an extra thirty minutes to thumb through before Mykala returned to the unit.

By then, James Potter was deader than a doornail.

The room had been ransacked, James' slippers were missing, and he was lying on the couch in a very unnatural position, with his head and upper torso sprawled over the armrest, as if someone had tried unsuccessfully to pull him off.

Mykala Rashon Washington had a choice to make. Death on the unit was not all that uncommon. When it happened naturally, the doctor was called in, and the family was notified that they had three days to remove their family member's possessions and vacate the premises. If they left anything, Meadowdale would dispose of it however they chose.

If she rearranged the room quickly and pulled James back on the couch, it would be an easy call to make. However, if this was not a natural death, and the coroner found out, it would mean her job.

Taking a deep breath, Mykala decided to clean up the room. But, before she could act, Nurse Bernice came through the door and demanded angrily, "Miss Mykala, where have you been? There are buzzers going off all down this hall!"

Mykala turned guiltily, her dark complexion flushing to mahogany, just as Nurse Bernice Henshaw saw Potter's body. "What the devil? What happened here?"

"I just came in myself," stammered Mykala. "He was like that and the room looks like someone was looking for something. I don't think this is natural."

"Obviously," sneered Nurse Bernice. "We have to call the doctor, and the administrator, Mr. Khan. This doesn't look good for any of us."

As they left the room, Nurse Bernice closed the door and placed a chair in front of it, to prevent anyone from accidently entering until the doctor arrived.

"Now, see about the other guests, Mykala, while I make

the necessary calls," Nurse Bernice said in a much gentler tone. She realized it would be better if the aide was not upset.

Coming down the hall toward them was Olive, with a pair of slippers in her hand. "I found these by our door. I think they belong to James Potter," Olive said, handing them to Mykala. "Why is there a chair in his door? Did something happen?"

"Thank you, Mrs. Harting. Just go back to your room. Everything is fine." Nurse Bernice's lips were in a thin, hard line and her eyes belied her statement. Mykala handed the slippers to Nurse Bernice, and then hurried down the hall to where two rooms had red lights flashing.

The buzz in Olive's brain was a warning that something was afoot. And she intended to find out just what it was.

Potter's roommate, Howard Dutt, had recently been moved to LaRhonda, and Potter seemed to be the next to transfer to the third floor, the road to no return. But this death was not normal.

Walter was asleep, so Olive put on her tweed jacket once again and went to the glass door on the east side, leading to the gardens.

As she punched in the security code, she thought about the strange way Nurse Bernice had acted, and how nervous Mykala looked.

The sky was studded with stars, in spite of the glow of city lights. It always made her relax a bit to imagine that somewhere up there, someone on another planet in another galaxy was looking down at Earth twinkling in the Milky Way and thinking similar thoughts.

It took away some of the strangeness of this place and

time. And, Olive had to admit, living at Meadowdale was strange in its own way.

This was the first time they had allowed a woman to live on the unit, although most of the nurses and aides were female. At first they were a little hostile, then accepting, and now they counted on her to notify them of problems, or to help the more mobile men on Windom.

Olive's presence was a blessing when the staff was stretched beyond their limits with men who might be talking to a potted plant or swatting at invisible aliens.

Helping with a game of dominoes or sorting the puzzle pieces was something Olive could do while the aide helped a guest to the showers. Keep a man seated at the table in the small dining room or shepherding a wandering soul back to his room lifted some of the workload on the busy aides. Olive had become a fixture on Windom.

Olive congratulated herself for becoming indispensible as she walked from the patio with the plastic chairs and little round table to the path which cut through the small, lush lawn to the gardens.

These were the gardens shown in the brochure featuring beautiful foliage and colorful flower beds, landscaped by a group of Master Gardeners.

She walked the path through the flowers led to a lovely walled prayer garden. There, a large statue of St. Francis of Assisi stood before a glistening water feature wall. Handsome carved wooden benches were positioned on the cobblestones of this small retreat. Olive knew from the brochure this would be her favorite spot of all.

In reality, the patio was the only place Olive could take Walter because it actually had a place to sit.

Unlike the photo in the brochure, the serene prayer garden with the low stone wall had no furniture. A few months earlier one of the "guests" had piled up the wooden benches and made an escape over the east wall by the covered parking lot.

Mr. Juneaux was found about four miles away, heading for the railroad tracks. He had been an engineer on the MKT railroad in his younger days and when he heard the wail of the locomotive, tried his best to get back to work. He was moved to another facility, far from the sound of trains, planes and maybe even automobiles.

For almost the first time Olive was acutely aware that the gardens had been elevated over the first floor. She could faintly hear sounds of a dishwasher, and metallic rattling of pots and pans. Olive surmised the prayer garden sat directly over the kitchen in the back of the main floor.

Olive shook her head as she remembered her first impression of Meadowdale. She naively embraced a peaceful retirement perfect for active senior adults.

There <u>were</u> senior adults playing cards or on computers in the library on her visit. She actually envisioned joining them when Walter was resting.

There was a list of various activities posted in hall by the door of the dining room that piqued her interest.

However, according to that blasted Contract, "guests" on the second floor could not fraternize with the Indies or go to Julep. She was a second floor resident with Walter. So, no pool, no pets. And of course, no cigarettes.

She had looked longingly through the glass doors, into a well-appointed dining hall which accommodated up to sixty guests at a time. Two ladies had entered, laughing and commenting on the delicious meal they were to share at lunch.

Olive then gazed down the brightly lit hall to the right where each door was decorated by the occupant. "These must be the single Indie apartments," Olive had thought to herself.

If she had continued down the hall, around the corner was a covered breezeway that led to large, shared apartments. There golf carts were parked for residents to use to access the pool, theater or rehab center at Julep.

Eighteen months ago, she had sat down with the Administrator, Fawad Khan to go over the Contract. He was a piece of work, thought Olive at the time, reprovingly.

Khan's large office area faced an alcove with Conyers and cockatiels in a large cage. Visitors found them charming, but Khan hated them. His secretary was in charge of feeding them, a task she disliked almost as much as she disliked Khan himself.

Although Khan had tried to steer Olive to Julep for herself, with Walter on Windom, she convinced him that a shared room on Windom would serve them both very well. He also tried to have her move their Estate Planning to Rest Assured, and use Smith Funeral Home.

Olive just smiled and told him her Trust handled it very well. Her strong personality and persistent pressure made him throw up his hands and finalize the contract as she demanded.

Coming back to the present, Olive realized that appearance could be deceiving. Meadowdale was not idyllic, and she and Walter would not be doing any of the activities on the list downstairs. Like many other seniors, she felt her life narrowing.

Olive shivered slightly, but not from the cold. Quickly she returned to the warmth of Windom Hall, hung up her jacket, and settled into the recliner next to Walter. He was dozing peacefully to the muted sounds of "The Late Night Show."

So far Walter had been able to get around, and his dementia was mainly a benign loss of present realities. He knew her, and loved her. His wit and playful spirit remained, and endeared him to the staff. But slowly the disease was progressing.

Today it was Windom Hall. Tomorrow it could be LaRonda, called "the Last Roundup" by the staff. Rumor was if a "guest" went there, soon they would take the final trip to the next level, a stairway to heaven

Olive wondered if James Potter was climbing those stairs right now, and who had put him on that path? She had found his slippers, but what other clues had Olive missed, she pondered. It was time to find out.

CHAPTER 5

Olive picked up her pink princess phone and punched in Laurel's number. They had become fast friends since Martin arrived on the Unit and Laurel had installed the VHS player.

One of the old black and white comedies featured Laurel and Hardy. When the aides saw it, they thought it was Laurel and Harting, and so dubbed the two women who hung out on the porch on Saturdays, talking and laughing while their husbands dozed.

Although Laurel was nearly twenty years Olive's junior, they both loved books, world affairs and philosophical debate. James Potter's death smacked of both mystery and mistakes.

The shift change came at 11 pm. Although it was 11:30, Nurse Bernice had to wait until both Dr. Patel, the staff physician, and Mr. Khan drove in for this emergency meeting.

Olive had positioned Walter at one of the tables not far from Potter's room, and had a domino game going when Doctor Patel arrived. A frowning Mr. Khan came striding through the door a few minutes later, looking angry for being called in on his day off.

Nurse Bernice greeted them both and led them to Room 213, moving the chair from in front of the closed door.

"This is how the room was when Mykala discovered him. She was clearing away the trays from the hall," Bernice explained.

"What time was that?" asked Dr. Patel as he bent over the body, now stiff from Rigamortis.

"I think it was about eight pm?" said Nurse Bernice, in an uncertain tone.

"Is Mykala here?" he inquired.

"No, shift changes at eleven," said Nurse Bernice, "so she went on home."

"Well, we will need to talk to all the staff tomorrow when they come on at three in the afternoon." Noting it was Sunday, Mr. Khan said briskly, "I don't know if it is all the same staff. Do I need to call in those who were here tonight?"

"Absolutely," said Dr. Patel. "I don't feel right about putting 'Natural Causes' on the certificate until I am sure."

Mr. Khan's frown deepened and he looked worried, Olive noted. Looking up at the ceiling while he cleared his throat, Khan thought for a minute. Then, he looked hard at Dr. Patel, as if willing a different outcome. "What else could it be, Doctor? He was old. He obviously had another heart attack and nearly threw himself off the couch. I really don't want to deal with an unnecessary autopsy with the family, uh, if it can be avoided."

Dr. Patel looked at Khan sharply. "Do you have the proper papers for a DNR and quick disposal of the body? Has the family approved any burial plans? If they have, we can move on this immediately. If not, I will have to follow all the proper procedures."

Nurse Bernice hurried off to look through the files just as Walter told Olive, "Time for my drinkie dear. I need a vanilla drinkie."

Suddenly Dr. Patel and Mr. Khan were aware of Olive and Walter. "We will of course handle this properly and with all the respect due the resident," Mr. Khan said, his appearance making a sudden shift. His insincere smile and prayerful hands seemed phony to Olive, as Mr. Khan nodded in her direction.

Dr. Patel and he moved to the nurse's station to look over the papers Nurse Bernice had found.

"Rats," Olive said. "Where?" Walter asked, looking around with curiosity. "Oh, I thought I saw one down here by the ice machine, but I was wrong."

She took his arm, smiling up at him as she had for their 60 years of marriage. They moved down to the refrigerator and got his Ensure and headed back to their room.

The next day Olive was up bright and early. Walter was sleeping in, as he often did. His days and nights were turned around, which meant she would need a quick nap before shift change if she was to find out anything more about poor Mr. Potter.

At three sharp, the staff arrived. Nurse Bernice Henshaw, Chantel Parks, Calista Boudreaux and Mykala Washington were waiting for Dr. Patel and Mr. Khan at the Nurse's station. "Is this everyone?" Mr. Khan asked?

"No, I haven't been able to get hold of Tia Marie," said Nurse Bernice. "She is supposed to work today and tomorrow since Monday is laundry day.

"I asked Chantel if there was anything missing from Mr. Potter's room, and she said $100 in tens, and his retirement watch. Does anyone know about those items?" Mr. Khan asked.

"Well," said Calista putting her hand on her ample hip, "that man was always countin' his money. I mean, he has had those same ten dollar bills for the last three years. Every day he would count them and tell me one day they would be mine."

"He promised them to me too," exclaimed Mykala, her big hoop earrings flashing. "And that watch was really expensive. It's gone?"

"And so is Tia Marie," said Nurse Bernice smugly.

"When do you pick up the trays on the 200 hall?" asked Mr. Khan.

"Usually around seven, but last night I had to get gas in my car so I left to fill my tank and started a little late," Mykala said nervously, pushing her hands into her scrub's pockets and looking away from the hard gaze of the administrator.

"So Tia Marie could have found him dead, rifled through his drawers and taken his watch and money and run off," postulated Mr. Khan. "I think we have solved the mystery. What do you think, Dr. Patel?"

"Since you have the "Do not resuscitate" and an order to cremate, I believe we can proceed. Let the family know Mr. Potter died of natural causes and we will handle moving the body to Smith Funeral Home. The storage people can come clean out his room and take things from there." Dr. Patel seemed relieved to have the incident settled.

Nurse Bernice queried quietly, "Should we try to find Tia Marie, or at least hold her last check?"

"I don't think that will be a problem," said Mr. Khan. "I doubt if she will be asking for it, but if she does, act as if nothing has happened. We don't want word to get out. Just don't give her any references from us."

No one noticed the chubby afternoon aide, Amy Armstrong, gather all the unused medication for James Potter and slip it into her oversized Coach bag. She checked "disposed of properly" on the chart and placed it back on the medicine cart.

She then hurried to punch the code into the elevator panel and went down to her locker in the employee lounge. There she quickly changed into black tights, a red and black plaid skirt, oversized black sweater and knee high black boots. Amy stopped at the bathroom in the main hall to quickly spray her short, spiky hairdo again and reapply her bright red lipstick. Suddenly she bounded out the door to catch her connection.

Dr. Patel would not notice since he only came when called, and Nurse Bernice would be too busy getting the shift aids sent out on their tasks, she thought.

"I may be able to score something good from the Pharmacist with this stuff," she chortled as she did a jig at her old grey Hyundai then drove away in a swirl of autumn leaves.

Amy smiled in the rearview mirror, rubbing a blob of Raunchy Red off her front tooth. It is an ill wind that blows no good to anyone.

CHAPTER 6

Unlike in the general population, death was a fairly common event in the Memory Care Unit at Meadowdale Manor. All of the guests were in some stage of dementia and none would recover.

Mr. Chester D'Wores moved into room 213, followed by another roommate, Mr. Arthur Corbin, who had transferred from Julep. Things quickly went back to normal, or as normal as they ever were.

Olive and Walter went for their morning walk in the courtyard, and made a quick detour into the prayer garden. The serenity drew Olive and her sturdy shoes were adequate for the uneven cobblestones, but they were difficult for Walter, who was not very steady on his feet anymore.

Olive regretted that the lovely carved benches had been removed due to Mr. Juneaux's escape. When they turned to go back to the patio, Walter stumbled, and then toppled, hands splayed outward.

Bebe Tron was watching from the window. She hurried out to see if Walter was okay.

"Can you help me lift him?" asked Olive querulously. "No Missy Harting. We cannot touch the patient. If he is broken, we call the ambulance. I so sorry Missy. If he is cut, you take him to Infirmary. Otherwise, you handle it," Bebe explained.

The Infirmary wasn't really for anything other than mild illness or hospice. Anything that required actual medical attention meant a visit to the nearby hospital. Charges of $100 a day applied at the Infirmary, plus the daily charge for the room. It wasn't worth the hassle.

Olive snapped at Bebe, "Then bring me his walker from our room. I'll wait here with Walter." With some difficulty Olive got Walter to his feet and into the plastic chair on the patio.

"Are you hurt dear?" she inquired nervously, checking his head. Walter showed her a scrape on his hand and Olive, clutching her pearls to her to her chest, breathed a sigh of relief.

When Bebe returned with the walker, Olive thanked her and said, "Stop by my room later please." Then she and Walter slowly walked back into the Unit.

Walter sat back in his recliner and slouched into his usual position for a nap, hands resting on the arms of the chair and his head tilted to one side. Olive removed his outdoor shoes and slipped the old grey house shoes on him.

As she did, it reminded her that Potter's slippers had been by her door. Why had they been left by her door? His room was two doors down. If Potter had a heart attack, why would he have brought the slippers to her door? Something wasn't right.

Tia Marie was such a sweet girl. She worked four days a week, doing the laundry for many of the guests, cleaning the Unit before family visited on the weekends, and was very tidy. The state of Potter's room was anything but orderly when he died.

Olive called Laurel. "I can't stop thinking about Potter and the way things were done. I also can't believe Tia Marie had anything to do with it," Olive said to Laurel. "The drawers were ransacked, the room was a mess, and Potter's slippers were by my door! Something is fishy."

"Did the family say anything?" asked Laurel.

"Oh, I think it was some cousin or nephew who rarely saw the old man, and he really didn't care. I don't think they even are having a funeral for him. Smith just cremated the remains and the relative paid the people from Load and Lock Storage to dispose of the things in the room."

"Paid for the removal of the furniture? When did that start?"

Olive had to smile. "Laurel, apparently he didn't realize you don't have to pay for that, but Mr. Khan accepted the check with alacrity."

"I have to file this deposition. Gotta go, but let me know what you find out about Potter," Laurel said as she hung up. The law office where she worked was small, but busy. Its Mockingbird location was a bit of a drive from her apartment, but close to Meadowdale.

There was a knock at the door. Olive opened to let Bebe in.

"Yes Missy Olive? You want talk to me?"

"Yes Bebe. You see, Tia Marie was supposed to do some extra laundry for me, some delicates, you understand. I haven't seen her today and she is always here on Thursdays." Olive offered her a cookie from the plate she was holding.

Bebe shook her head in refusal. Then she said, "Oh

Missy Olive, she gone. She leave and don't come back. New lady, Pat Baldwin, here now. You want I send her to you?" Bebe seemed nervous.

"No dear, but why did Tia Marie leave?" Olive persisted.

"Don't know, but she not happy here. The others gave her bad work, hard work. I think she was getting new work, better work," Bebe explained. "She good girl. She didn't do the bad thing Nurse said. She legal, with a real number and a boyfriend."

"Thank you Bebe," said Olive kindly. She reached into her pocket and pulled out a folded bill and handed it to Bebe.

"Here is five dollars, a little gift for helping me with the walker. I appreciate it so much," Olive said with a smile. "And, if you hear anything about the missing money or watch from poor old Mr. Potter, will you be sure and tell me? He was such a dear man and Walter and I miss him."

"Yes Missy Olive. I will tell you," whispered Bebe conspiratorially. She looked relieved now she knew where the interview was headed. "We all worry too. Something not right, but we can do nothing."

As Olive closed the door, she realized she had not paid close enough attention to all that was happening at Meadowdale Manor after all. Suddenly certain things began to fall into place.

She thought about the administrator and the way he handled Mr. Potter. And Dr. Patel, who rarely came on the unit except for emergencies. He seemed nervous about calling it natural causes, but obviously he wanted to please Khan. Something was up.

But now, it wasn't going to be her. She would nap while Walter dozed. Tonight he would again and again want to get a "drinkie" and she needed to be alert. Olive Greyn Harting, reporting for duty!

CHAPTER 7

On Saturday, Laurel arrived early with a laundry basket of clean clothes for Martin.

That onerous "Contract" had been filled with fine print, as to what was covered and what was not.

The contract had a choice between the facility doing daily laundry, or the family doing it weekly. Laurel's choice was made by her financial situation. Daily laundry specified the staff was not to use a laundry basket, meaning that only small loads were done.

Again, money seemed the driving force at Meadowdale Manor, not the best for the "guest".

Working for attorneys had made Laurel very aware of the fine print. That was how she knew that when a guest moved, or left the premises for more than three days, the room had to be cleared, either by the family or the facility.

Sitting very erect in her tweed jacket and brown slacks, Olive was busy at a table in the small dining room writing letters where Walter would not add his marks on them. Laurel joined her.

"Olive, I just passed the Load and Lock truck in the parking lot. I noticed that it is always Load and Lock Storage that comes in to empty the rooms. I thought the family had a choice?" Laurel asked, pulling up a chair and setting her water bottle on the table.

Olive sighed. "In fact, it is the Markowitz brothers. I won't say they are greedy, but Khan steers people to Load and Lock, which is under the Markowitz umbrella. So is the Pill Box Pharmacy, which the doctors here use. I don't know what other pies they have their fingers in, but obviously there are a few."

Olive went on, "I'm sure they didn't ask you, since you made it obvious you did not have a nest egg, but they tried to steer me to Rest Assured. It is a kind of Annuity or estate planning that seems geared to guests without interested relatives."

Laurel took a sip of water and asked with curiosity, "How would that work?"

"If there is no family member, or none that is involved, then the annuity pays for the funeral, burial, and headstone of the guest. It also covers the cost of removing the items left. Guests are encouraged to name a charity for any remaining finances."

Olive smiled wryly and reminded Laurel, "Of course, in a case like mine, my son Gordon will either inherit, or be responsible for all the bills I leave."

Getting up from the table, Olive collected her papers. "Come to my room and bring Martin when you are done," Olive demanded firmly.

Soon Laurel and Martin arrived. Martin was unusually alert and smiling. He greeted Olive with a sideways hug and shook Walter's hand.

"Glad to meet you," he said cordially, proffering his hand as if meeting Walter for the first time.

"Same here," responded Walter, shaking it vigoriously.

Walter leaned back in his recliner while Laurel got Martin to sit down in the other. Olive turned on "Thomas the Train" and handed out raspberry sugar-free popsicles to the men.

"If we are really good," Walter whispered loudly, "we can have some real ice cream later."

"What's up?" asked Laurel as she followed Olive to the other side of the curtain.

Olive sat on her single bed, and Laurel perched on a side chair.

"Bebe told me they found Potter's money in a shoe in Bobby's room. They still haven't found the watch. I think Bobby was involved in Potter's death."

"What would they do to him if that were true?" Laurel asked, her brow furrowed with concern. "He isn't capable of making rational decisions, and he can't be held responsible."

"I know, but if he can be violent, he is a danger to the rest of us."

"I can't believe he would do anything deliberately," Laurel replied, dismissing the idea immediately. "But I guess it is worth watching. What about the Tia Marie theory?"

"Apparently she found a better job. I am glad for her," assured Olive. "Anyway, let's get back to our guys before Thomas gets off the track." They both laughed and went back to find both men sound asleep, sticky popsicle sticks dropped casually on the floor.

Laurel thought Walter looked like a cherub, with his round, chubby cheeks and thinning, snow white hair spilling over his forehead. It seemed a shame he never had the farm he dreamed about, although he always tried some kind of agricultural experiment according to Olive.

"Tell me about your backyard menagerie again," said Laurel.

Since the men were dozing soundly, Laurel and Olive moved to the tables in the visitor's lounge. Olive's eyes became softer as she retreated into pleasant memories.

"Well, we had a lovely home on a large lot so Walter decided that rabbits would be the perfect money-making project. They don't take up much space and he could sell their meat to the Mexican meat market. At least, that was his plan."

"We had 12 cages, three bucks and nine does of various kinds and colors. He liked the Silky ones, the Lops, and of course the New Zealand White which are good for meat. He invested in the proper water bottles, heavy pottery food dishes, and had books on rabbit farming."

"Of course, the rabbit population exploded. Eventually we ended up with thirty-two rabbits, and it became a full-time job."

"Then, Gordon, our son, was in a car accident, so we had to take care of him for about a week. We asked a neighbor lady to watch the rabbits while we were gone. Walter promised her two rabbits as payment."

"When we got home, Walter asked Mrs. Brooks, our neighbor, which rabbits she wanted. She carefully pointed out a beautiful full-sized black buck and a sweet white silky doe that was able to be held and stroked."

Walter explained he would bring them over later. Meanwhile, Mrs. Brooks hurried home and got her little cage set up for her new pets.

"About four in the afternoon Walter arrived at her door with two skinned rabbits as a thank you gift. When she opened the door, Mrs. Brooks stood in shock."

"Here are your rabbits," Walter proudly said, with the raw carcasses dangling from his outstretched hand.

Quickly gathering her wits, Mrs. Brooks inquired, "Which is the black one and which is the white one?"

Laurel laughed at the visual of poor Mrs. Brooks, who had anticipated her own little brood of beautiful bunnies.

Life was full of unpleasant surprises. And what Laurel and Olive didn't know, there were more to come at Meadowdale.

CHAPTER 8

Mr. Phillips had been in Room 209 less than a year. It was a room he had shared with Bob Walker. Poor Bob had a wild psychotic episode. Walker ran around the shared room, tripping over the chairs, running into the wall, and ended up splayed out by the commode.

When Bob came to, he was lethargic and listless. Dr. Patel advised Walker be transferred to LaRonda, "The Last Roundup."

Dr. Patel usually spent his time with the wealthy widows in the Independent Living area. His bedside manner kept them happy, and their adoration satisfied an emptiness in him. Every sniffle, every headache, every whiny complaint was an excuse for Dr. Patel to go to the privacy of their room and give them his undivided attention.

Unless it was really urgent, Dr. Patel turned over the care of those guests in the Assisted Living to Dr. Punjab, and the Memory Care units to Dr. Singh. LaRonda usually was in the care of expert nursing staff or Hospice.

Since Albert Phillips was fairly alert, comparatively, Olive often invited him to join in a game of 42. Albert seemed to understand where to place the dominoes, unlike

Walter who sometimes built roads or walls with the pretty black tiles.

Although Albert was on Windom Hall, he actually was fairly able to take care of himself. That is, when he wasn't confused and looking for a way out so he could go home.

His daughter, Carol, had complained of his behavior when he lived with her. He was restless, agitated, and often ranted about the IRS trying to get to his money. When he accused her of trying to do the same, she placed him in a group home run by a Registered Nurse.

It was a licensed facility, with three other men. The cost was nearly $4,000 a month, but it was less than many larger facilities. However, he had "escaped" three times, even with a coded door, alarm and ankle bracelet. Albert was clever and capable.

In desperation Carol cashed in his life insurance policy and paid for six months in advance at Meadowdale Manor. It was the final stop for Albert. But medication helped, and he was usually affable around others.

Albert liked to drop in to see Martin, and their love of old movies made them fast friends.

"Well Pilgrim," Albert drawled, "I see you are back on the range. Isn't that my favorite cowboy, John Wayne, up there on the screen?"

"Yup," agreed Martin. "I think he is going to get the bad guys this time. Pull up a chair. I'll ring for that big gal to bring us some popcorn and we can enjoy the matinee."

The two of them settled into the two recliners. Charles Gordon turned over in bed so his back was to them. "Rednecks," he muttered to himself, "I wish they would both drop dead."

If wishes were fishes all dreamers would eat.

Laurel and Olive sat in the visitor's room while Walter dozed back at their room. Laurel had been restless all afternoon, concerned with Martin's declining health. She needed someone to talk to, and Olive was the only friend she could confide in.

"You know, Olive, Martin had been big in the music publishing industry in the '80's and '90's. When the record stores began closing, he went on his own, and things slowed way down. That's when I noticed he was having problems with the accounting, and also with his memory."

"It hadn't been that hard with Martin at first. I used green duck tape to lead to the coffee pot, and yellow with arrows to bring him back to the bedroom. He always brought me coffee in bed every morning." Laurel smiled at the memory."

"Our condo had a nice patio with a wooden gate, so I put a fake latch at the top where he could see it, and the real one down low. He would fiddle with it for several minutes, then give up and go back into the house to "work" or sit in one of the rockers and rest."

"Then, the hallucinations and wandering started. In the morning he seemed pretty normal and would go to his bedroom office to work on royalties, but by afternoon, nothing made sense to him. I still had to work, but I would go home at lunch to check on him."

"I might find him talking to the post on the patio. Once he invited it to lunch with us. More and more reality slipped away."

"In the evening, he never knew me so I wore an old grey

sweater with a nametag that said 'Ingrid' and became his caregiver. That way I could get him ready for bed."

"Adult day care wasn't a good fit. I couldn't leave him and I couldn't stay home. Things were not going well, and then he had a heart attack. I thought, "Assisted living, that's the ticket!" I called PLUM and the avalanche of calls, brochures and e-mails began."

"Martin didn't need activities and social events. He needed a secure unit where he could be safe. That's why Meadowdale was the perfect solution for us. He can't even manage the computer now, but he loves his old videos, and the staff is very kind to him."

"When we sold the condo, it didn't bother him because he was already past knowing or caring about the present reality. Martin is a kid again, and every day is Saturday at the cinema."

"Are you worried about his heart?" queried Olive.

"The doctor said the next one might take him," agreed Laurel, "but then, as long as he is happy, we take one day at a time." But Martin wasn't the one they needed to worry about.

CHAPTER 9

That evening after dinner Albert Phillips returned to room 209 and settled in his blue Naugahyde recliner. Feeling a bit chilly, he pulled the cozy green and orange afghan up to his chin and began to snooze.

About an hour later, as Mykala was making her rounds, picking up trays and helping her "men" into bed, she entered Albert's room, to find Bobby Turkle "The Turk" sitting on top of Albert.

Bobby made himself more comfortable by placing a pillow over Albert's head, as if Albert were part of the chair. Albert was struggling to push him off, but Bobby only wriggled his bottom more securely into Albert's lap and pushed his head firmly back on the pillow.

"Bobby!" Mykala hollered. "Get off Albert!" She reached for the buzzer to turn on the red light outside the room.

"Help me," she cried toward the door as she tugged at Bobby's arm to try and dislodge him from the chair.

He pushed back violently and Mykala fell hard to the floor, her head striking the end table.

Bobby's motion pushing Mykala was just enough to lift Bobby off Albert and cause the pillow to tumble onto the floor. Albert shook his head, gasping for air. His arms were locked beneath the afghan and he struggled to free himself.

Olive and Calista rushed into the room. While Olive helped Mykala to her feet, Calista jerked Bobby out of the recliner and shoved him roughly against the wall.

"What the hell do you think you are doing, Mr. Bobby? This ain't your room!" fumed Calista. He just looked at her angrily, "My room, my chair, my remote."

Mykala checked her head for blood, but her hand came away clean. She then pulled the afghan off of Albert and began to check him out. "I think we got here in time," she said turning to Calista. "I think this is what happened to that nice Mr. Potter."

"Well it ain't happening again," Calista scolded. "I don't care how much money this Mr. Bobby has, we don't sit on Mr. Albert!" She grabbed Bobby firmly by the arm and marched him back to his room. "I'll watch this one. Miss Olive, you go get Nurse Bernice. Let's get this settled right now. Mykala, you stay here with Mr. Albert and make sure he still breathing."

They could hear Calista loudly reprimanding Bobby all the way to Haliburton hall and his room. Wide-eyed, Albert struggled to get his breath while Mykala soothed him. "It's going to be all right Mr. Albert. Nurse will be here in a minute."

Nurse Bernice hurried to Albert Phillip's chair and took his pulse. As Nurse Bernice asked him questions, Albert seemed to be alert and coherent.

Olive stood quietly at the door. Finally things were beginning to make sense.

Obviously Bobby had done the same thing with Mr.

Potter, with disastrous results. How many "accidental deaths" had occurred this way? And, as with Potter, were they always written off as "natural causes"?

After moving Mr. Phillips to his bed and making him comfortable, Nurse Bernice called Dr. Patel. "Mr. Phillips, in room 209, has had an incident. I think he should be moved to the infirmary immediately." She nodded a few times, listening to the instructions on the other end. "Right, immediately." She affirmed.

Leaving Mykala and Olive with Mr. Phillips, Nurse Bernice went back to her station to start the process of moving Albert.

"What will happen to Bobby?" queried Olive.

"Don't know," Mykala shrugged. "It ain't the first time he has hurt someone on the Unit. If his daughter didn't bail him out he would have been gone long ago."

By ten o'clock, two orderlies had arrived with a gurney and whisked Albert Phillips away. He seemed confused but was not in distress.

When Olive got back to her room, Walter was just waking up from his "nap."

"Time for a drinkie, Sweetie?" he grinned. "Sure enough," Olive said, and they strolled down the hall to the alcove.

When Olive got up the next morning, Walter was in a good mood. It was shower time. A bouncy young aid, Marta Rivera, came in to get him.

"Good morning Walter. Ready for a shower?"

"You gonna shower with me," Walter said with a gleam in his eye.

"You bad boy!" she responded with a smile. "No, but you'll have a cleaner mind when we are done."

"Have you heard about Mr. Phillips?" Olive inquired.

"What about him?" asked Marta.

"How he is doing in the infirmary," said Olive impatiently.

"Oh, is he over there?" Marta shrugged dismissively and took Walter into the bathroom for his shower.

This is getting nowhere, Olive thought, and went out into the main room to find Rani.

She was busy at the Nurse's Station with paperwork.

"Miss Rani," asked Olive quietly, "How is Albert?"

"He is in the infirmary on Hospice," Rani sadly responded. "Poor Mr. Albert. The family has been called in."

"Really? He seemed okay last night when the orderlies came. What happened?"

"I'm not sure, but the notes were here when I arrived this morning. Load and Lock Storage came for his things. The family needs to make some decisions."

Olive noted in her journal what was happening. Things were occurring that just didn't look right. Who was pulling the strings? Was it the administrator, Khan? Was it Dr. Patel? Or, was it the Markowitz brothers?

Laurel had researched it through a legal assistant in the law firm. He found from their corporate records they not only owned Meadowdale Manor, but also had interests in a Load-N-Lock Storage and a Pill Box Pharmacy in each of the three cities where they had retirement housing.

Mr. Khan always recommended the Smith Funeral Home, but Laurel could find no legal connection with the

Markowitz brothers. Still, many fingers, many pies, and a pile of cash for dessert.

Olive didn't have time to be concerned about Albert, as Walter, fresh from the shower, was ready to have his breakfast. She settled him in the recliner with his tray table as Yvonne Chavez, a pretty young aide in bright yellow scrubs, came in.

"Ola Meester Walter," she warbled. "Here ees your lovely breakfast." Yvonne set down the tray with a flourish, patted Walter on the head and wiggled out of the room rumba-style. Walter had a smirk on his face. "See, Olive, she likes me."

"Yes dear," sighed Olive. "I'm sure she does."

Walter attacked his soggy eggs with a vengeance as Olive contemplated what might have happened to Albert Phillips.

Something was rotten in Denmark, make that Meadowdale, and Olive needed Laurel to help her find out what it was.

Or, perhaps that smell was just Walter, being a bad boy again. Olive saw him lift the left cheek of his buttock and loudly blast, then grin wickedly.

"It's these eggs fault," he explained, and laughed.

CHAPTER 10

The infirmary was a place of mystery at Meadowdale. Like Hotel California, guests checked in but they never checked out. Well, not "never." For simple illness or wound care, a guest might spend a night or two, but if it was serious, the guest was transported to a nearby hospital for actual treatment.

The usual stay was short for declining guests. Mr. Khan and Dr. Patel always suggested Hawthorn Hospice.

Usually the guest who ended up under the care of Hospice was from either the second or third floor. Their room was cleaned quickly to make way for a new guest, who paid a hefty price for the needed care. His room being cleared sealed the fate of Mr. Albert Phillips.

When Olive heard the whispers that Load and Lock had been called she became concerned. Dressing quickly, Olive looked in the mirror. Her deep brown eyes registered her worry. She ran her hand through her salt and pepper pixie and adjusted her glasses. "How can I find out what is really happening? I can't leave Walter to find out."

As she left the bathroom, she glanced over at her dear Walter, with his cherubic face. Even dozing he looked sweet.

Olive remembered how, when she was a serious student

working on her Master's degree, he would meet her at class to walk her to the car. Walter was a mathematics whiz and a grade behind her, but his affectionate nature counterbalanced her pragmatic focused attitude.

When Walter was awake, he always had a twinkle in his eye, and a pat for her backside if she got too close. And she liked to get too close.

Olive sat in her recliner and picked up her pink Princess phone and punched in Laurel's number.

"Laurel, we need to get into the infirmary to find out what is happening with Albert," Olive said in a low, conspiratorial tone. "Bring a disguise."

"I was heading out for church, but I can go this afternoon," Laurel said.

Two hours later Laurel arrived with a shopping bag containing a set of scrubs, a short, dark wig and heavy tennis shoes. She changed quickly into her disguise.

"Since it is Sunday they will probably have temps," explained Olive. "Just go in, collect the trash and put it in the green rolling bin by the back door. But, while you are in there, use your phone camera to take photos of as much as you can so we can see what is really going on."

Laurel twisted her long brown ponytail into a bun and pulled on the curly black wig. She slipped her phone into the brown scrub pants pocket and, making sure the coast was clear, headed for the back door. As she crossed the lawn to the Infirmary, she quickly slipped on blue rubber gloves, and opened the door.

An orderly was playing Free Cell on the office computer. He didn't even look around. Laurel went through the double doors into the hall, where she was faced with four closed doors.

The first door was locked, but through the reinforced window she could see a large cabinet with pharmaceutical supplies and medical instruments. Laurel snapped a photo through the glass. In the photo, it was difficult to recognize individual items in the room because the reinforcement in the glass resembled chicken wire across the photo. She took a second photo, but it was still unclear.

The second door opened to an examining room, with a gurney. She pulled the plastic bag of waste out, tied the top, and inserted a clean bag. Laurel pulled her cell phone from her pocket and took a quick photo of the cabinets. That photo was uninteresting but clear.

Frowning, Laurel looked around to make sure no one was aware her. The man at the desk was still playing a computer game and probably would not have noticed if the place was on fire. She continued down the corridor cautiously.

The third door yielded at her touch. Laurel stepped in to see a large, elderly woman dozing in the chair. "Must be Hospice," Laurel thought.

Albert, so alive a few days ago, lay silent in the bed, his mouth agape. His skin color was pasty white, and he looked terrible. His arms bore bruising from multiple injections, and two pill bottles were on the silver tray by the bed.

Laurel pulled out her cell phone and snapped photos of the labels on the two pill bottles. Then she riffled through the paperwork on the side table and snapped a photo of the one listing Albert's condition. Suddenly the heavy-set woman woke up.

"Who are you? What are you doing here?" the lady stood erect suddenly, put her hands on her hips, and demanded an answer from Laurel.

Laurel quickly slipped the cell phone in her pocket and pulled the trash bag out of the waste bin by the gurney and tied the top. "Just takin' out the trash, M'am. That fella looks pretty bad. Is he going to make it?"

"None of your business Missy. Just do your job and leave," the woman whispered, suddenly looking menacingly at Laurel. Laurel noticed Mr. Phillips didn't even stir at the disturbance.

"On my way," Laurel said breezily. She grabbed her two bags of trash and scurried out of the room. The orderly nodded absently as she passed, now working on a Roblox game.

Once outside, Laurel went behind the building and opened the bag from Albert's room. There were a few forms among the other waste, and she quickly retrieved them, retied the bag.

Lifting the heavy lid to the waste disposal bin she threw in the two bags she had collected. "And now I am a garbage collector," she thought to herself.

Once safely inside Olive's room, Laurel went into the bathroom to clean up and get back into her own clothes. She stashed the costume in her backpack and hid it behind the recliner.

"Well?" she asked Olive, handing her the cell phone.

Olive looked over the forms, and then at the photos in the phone. She enlarged the photos of the pill bottles and concentrated on the labels.

"Just as I suspected, they are using heavy pharmaceuticals

to incapacitate the poor man. I imagine they have something to make it look like a heart attack, and he will be out of there. Probably won't kill him, but if he makes it to the hospital, they can refuse to take him back, and his room will be free to lease to another well-paying guest without questions."

"What can we do to help, Olive?" concerned, Laurel was looking for answers.

"I'm not sure. We can see to it Carol has been alerted. Surely she cares about his well being enough to become actively involved. Why don't you meet with her and let her see the photos?"

Laurel considered it for a minute, then said, "But what will that accomplish? What if she doesn't believe us, or she doesn't care?"

"Then, not my monkey, not my circus," sighed Olive.

Laurel collected her backpack and went to Martin's room for her Sunday visit. He motioned to her to join him on the bed and smiled up at her.

"You are finally here. I haven't seen you in so long. I wish we could go home now, Lala." Martin reached for her hand and drew her down on beside him.

She lay next to him, her head on his chest and relaxed for the first time in weeks.

Later, when Mykala brought in trays for Charles and Martin, Laurel made sure Martin ate most of his food. The preformed riblets, mushy green beans and garlic bread were not exciting, but the cherry crumble looked tasty.

It was nearly seven pm when Laurel got home and called Carol. She and her husband had been out to dinner with friends and she was very tired when Laurel broached the problem of her father with her.

"What do you expect me to do? He was such a problem to find a place to take him, and now they let me know that his health is quickly failing. I am torn between sorrow and relief." Carol sounded a bit frazzled and defensive.

Laurel calmly explained, "We were there when the incident with Bobby Turkle happened. Your father was upset but not really hurt."

"What incident is that? When my father fell? Apparently they found him unconscious an hour later. I really don't care WHO found him and it doesn't matter now." Carol said harshly.

Laurel was stumped. "Fell? No, Bobby sat on him. I'm not sure what you were told," Laurel explained gently.

"Who are you again, and why are you calling me? Why are you interjecting yourself into my life? I have enough on my plate without this nonsense. My father is terminal. Hospice has been called. I am working with Meadowdale on final arrangements. They said it is a matter of hours." Her voice rose. "Please leave me alone or I will report you!"

Laurel softly sighed, "Sorry I bothered you. Your father was a special man. My condolences."

She hung up, very discouraged. Apparently the administration was protecting itself from any legal issues, but something smelled bad.

And it wasn't the monkey or the circus.

CHAPTER 11

Dr. Hardik Patel was finishing up the report on Mr. Phillips, which included Albert's fabled "fall" and the heavy costs of Hospice.

Dr. Patel's had a wife and four children who took trips back to India on a regular basis. This required creative billing to Medicare and Medicaid to cover his extra expenses. At Meadowdale, he had ample opportunity to pad the billing, with a large kick-back to Faward Khan the administrator.

The pharmaceutical companies also gave him generous perks for using their most expensive drugs, but now Khan was pressuring him for even more money. Khan's addiction to the casinos across the border in Oklahoma had added another layer of anxiety for Dr. Patel, who had always considered himself to be an honest and conscientious man.

Saul and Abe Markowitz seemed to turn a blind eye to any administrative tasks as long as the bottom line continued to be large and black. The beauty of raking in extra from the Pharmacy and storage buildings kept the brothers content.

The part-time aide Amy Armstrong was one of those women who earned the harsh looks from other women. She wore her scrubs a little tight and her makeup a little heavy. Her spiked blonde hairdo and pierced nose would have stood out anywhere. She stayed on the roster because she worked odd hours, did jobs no one else wanted.

Besides that, Dr. Patel stood up for her.

This day, Dr. Patel was bent over the chart at the nurse's station, making notations on several of them. He only came in on weekends if there was an unusual event. The accident with Mr. Phillips was one of those events.

Sliding up quietly to Dr. Patel, Amy put her hand on his shoulder.

"Since Mr. Phillips won't be back, may I check his room for any loose property before the family finishes clearing it out?"

He smiled at her, and grasped her hand in his, pulling her closer. "Yes, dear Amy. Do it quickly. He will be gone soon. Load and Lock has been notified, and the family is moving swiftly. Now, I will be in there in a few minutes to make sure you are alright." He smiled at her suggestively.

Their secret rendezvous was part of her charm. She would give Dr. Patel some small affection in return for rifling through the drawers and dressers of those who were leaving.

They never met outside of the unit. He never spoke of it to anyone, his hold over her. And she in turn, kept their secret.

Olive and Walter were seated in the corner of the dining room. She watched as Amy quickly went into Mr. Phillips room, followed in about five minutes by Dr. Patel.

Olive remained quiet, making sure she didn't disturb her dozing spouse. Within eight minutes Dr. Patel came out, wiping off bright red lipstick from the side of his neck.

A few moments later Amy came out, her spiked hair a little more mussed, looking triumphant.

Amy went straight to the medication cart and removed several pill bottles, slipped them in her pocket, and headed toward the elevator.

Suddenly a few more pieces to the puzzle fell into place. Olive wondered why she hadn't been aware of it before. "I am an old fool. Now I must be a careful old fool," thought Olive.

Sitting in her darkened apartment with some soft jazz playing, Laurel sipped a hot mug of Earl Grey tea, sweetened with a bit of honey. Laurel thought about what Carol had said. It made her sad, but there was nothing they could do.

Picking up her cell phone, Laurel called Olive to let her know that Carol was not at all interested in their help with her father. In fact, the information she had been fed made her antagonistic to their interference.

"I am not surprised," Olive remarked. "With what I have just seen, the guests who are most likely to enter Hospice are those with relatives who prosper most at their demise.'"

"I read about a young man in Indiana who had his uncle sign over his social security benefits and also he became a signer on the uncle's bank account. He then persuaded the staff that his uncle was aggressive, so the uncle was given heavy doses of antipsychotic drugs. Within a short time he became lethargic and unable to even feed himself and soon after died. The nephew inherited a great deal."

"Carol isn't at fault, but with the problems she had placing her father, it apparently was easier to believe a convenient falsehood than to face an uncomfortable truth as to her father's care."

Laurel just shook her head in disgust.

"I guess we just forget about dear Albert and take care of our own." Laurel was thinking about how much Martin needed her loving care.

So much had transpired in a short week.

Laurel was in as tight a spot as Carol had been. At this point, Laurel didn't dare rock the boat and go to the Administration about Patel and Amy. Retaliation would be fearful if they were involved in the fraud, and if not, Martin's care could be compromised.

When Martin was a younger man, his crown of white, curly hair had been dark blonde, and his pale blue eyes had been sharp enough to catch an error in a famous singer's royalties. The results had been a windfall of $5,000 to him, and more than $30,000 to his boss.

Now his eyes were vacant much of the time, and although he had a notebook filled with old royalty statements, they were just something for him to thumb through to pass time. The meaning was gone, as was the money.

The next evening Laurel arrived at Meadowdale after dinner had been served. She looked at the tray. It had been a decent meal. On the plate were the remains of lasagna, orange jello salad with shredded carrots, sweet corn and wheat bread.

Apparently there was also some kind of cookie, but both Charles and Martin had eaten theirs and nothing left but crumbs on the plate, and on their shirts.

Olive came in and sat in Charles' recliner while Laurel pulled a chair up next the recliner where Martin was snuggled under a blue and white Dallas Cowboy's afghan.

Olive leaned back. "Tell me about Martin. How did

he get into music publishing? That is such an interesting profession."

Laurel closed her eyes, remembering how it began. Then she motioned to the autographed NMPA award for 25 years membership. Smiling at Olive, she began.

"Martin had been raised on a farm in Union Valley, Texas. His goal as a young man was to get as far away from cows and corn as possible.

"Moving to Southern California and getting a Master's Degree at Pepperdine was the fulfillment of that dream. Because he was trustworthy, loyal and honest, he won a spot with a big-time producer in Hollywood."

"That is how he became a successful music publisher. I was working at a law firm that specialized in the music business. When Martin stopped to see Mr. Levine, he saw me. He always said my eyes reminded him of the song, "Blue Eyes Crying in the Rain.'"

"Ten years ago his mother died and left Martin the farm. Our kids were grown, so we sold our little bungalow in Mission Hills, California and moved to the home place in Union Valley. That's a wide place in the road here in Texas."

"We have two children. Jewel and her husband live in Indiana with their two children. He objects to the music business as being immoral. She hasn't been to see us since we moved."

"Our son Derreck is a Sushi chef. I tease him that he isn't a cook since he doesn't actually cook sushi. He lives in Los Angeles. He has been out one time because it is hard to get away, but he stays in touch."

"Most of our friends are still out there, except Richard Gerard, who lives here in Dallas. He has come by a couple of times, but I hate for anyone to see Martin since he has changed so much from the smart, funny and creative man he was."

"It feels so strange. I was enjoying sleuthing, but perhaps we should stop. I mean, we can't afford to be booted out. I think our snooping days are over."

"Oh no they aren't," Olive replied adamantly. "There are things going on all over the country in nursing homes that are really scary. We can't save Albert, but maybe we can prevent harm to someone else. What you don't know about growing old <u>can</u> kill you."

"In my free time, of which I seem to have much today," Olive said, "I researched nursing home problems on the internet. You would be shocked to know that in the past nursing homes had more injuries than miners or construction workers." Laurel sat back, interested in where Olive was headed.

Olive continued, "A lot of younger people don't seem to care, but since the corporate nursing homes have become big business, it has gotten worse. One day the boomers will all be here."

"What are some of the problems?" Laurel asked.

"It isn't just the food, which is not the greatest. Some of the major problems are with medication. Sometimes the patients were over medicated or given the wrong medication. The other problem is when patients are being moved," Olive said.

"Not all aides are properly trained, or strong enough to move patients. They can be dropped or pulled up wrong when transferred from a wheelchair to a bed. We are talking broken legs, arms pulled out of the socket, real injuries. Facilities don't like reporting these injuries."

Laurel interjected, "I've heard of nursing homes where residents were left sitting in their own urine or soiled clothing for hours. I know that state-trained advocates have to cover too many facilities to be effective, but they try to intervene."

Olive shook her head. "I haven't seen any abuse here at Meadowdale. There may be "white collar" offenses, like when Khan goes off to the Casinos a couple of times a month, and Dr. Patel fobs off his duties on Dr. Singh and Dr. Punjab unless it is some kind of incident that has to be reported."

"I bet he bills for it, though," said Laurel knowingly. "I check my Explanation of Benefits and he usually adds a charge on any procedure."

Laurel looked at her watch. "I have to go. I appreciate our friendship."

She hugged Olive and headed out.

As Olive walked back down the dimly lit hall to her room, she wondered how Khan and Patel could be scamming the system. It was time to be even more vigilant.

Entering the room, Olive settled back in her wing-back chair, glancing over at Walter, who was just waking up from another nap.

She held close the memories of her sweet Walter and how loving and kind he had been during their long years of marriage. She was the fire, and he was the quiet warmth of the family.

"I am ready for a walk and a drinkie," Walter said cheerily. "Are you ready dear Olive? It would be so nice. So nice. Just a sweet little drinkie before bedtime."

Olive looked at the clock. It was 10:20 am, yes, bedtime. Olive stood up and helped Walter out of his recliner. "Oh yes, Walter. A little walk, a little drinkie, and then we head for bed."

CHAPTER 12

Getting out of her beat up grey Hyundai, Amy straightened up her mini skirt and pulled her filmy blouse further down over her curvy hips so more cleavage would show. She then casually strolled into the Pill Box Pharmacy and went over to the cosmetic section as if deeply interested in eye shadows.

The stooped, balding pharmacist turned slightly to acknowledge Amy's presence as he assisted an elderly woman with her medication.

"Now, you need to remain upright for at least 30 minutes and drink two glasses of water when you take this Fosomax, Mrs. Wright. And you only take it once a week, always the same day at the same time," Vincent Rupert said loudly.

Mrs. Wright serenely smiled. "I'll tell Sadie, my daughter. She will make sure I take it right. Thank you again Mr. Rupert." Mrs. Wright took the small paper sack and waddled out the door, the bell dinging as it closed.

"Okay Amy, what do you have for me today?" Mr. Rupert, rubbing his hands eagerly.

"Just some Prozac, Xanax, Tramadol and Ativan," Amy said, smugly. "Some of it is almost all there. We've had two deaths, one on my unit and one of the Julep building. My friend Frances scoped that one out."

"Did you pay her for them?" he asked quickly.

"No, just traded her some oxycodone I got from Alex. Don't worry, she won't tell."

"Let me see them," he said. "Quickly, before anyone comes in."

Amy pulled out six pill bottles and a blister pack and handed to Mr. Rupert over the counter. He examined them, putting one bottle aside, and setting the other five in a drawer below her line of sight. He then looked closely at the blister pack.

"Amy, this one isn't even mine, and there are too few to make it worth it. And, that bottle is out of date, way out of date. Be sure and check them more carefully," he scolded. "How about one hundred dollars."

It wasn't a question. Amy bit her lip and looked up with fluttering eyelashes. "Can you make it one fifty?" she asked coquettishly.

"Nope. One hundred is it. If you can get me some morphine, that would be good. They shorted me on the last order and I could use it." Mr. Rupert counted out five twenties and turned back to the shelf behind him, effectively dismissing Amy.

Just then the door dinged and a woman with a child in tow came in. Amy shoved the money into her brown Coach bag, gave Mr. Rupert a sharp look and left.

Back at Meadowdale, Olive was deep in thought that evening when Laurel arrived. She just smiled at Laurel, who gave her a swift hug.

Laurel went down the hall to see Martin, who was dozing as Hopalong held the villain at gunpoint on the DVD.

Charles turned over to look at her. "He had another bad day," he whispered. "I think they gave him a heavy dose of meds to quiet him down. He doesn't like the new aide that fed him."

Laurel's eyes misted over and she knelt beside the chair, stroking Martin's arm. "Poor guy. I don't know if he even is aware of much anymore."

"Just don't transfer him to LaRonda Unit. The aides call it the "Last Roundup" because they keep them all sedated so it is less work. Just a warehouse until they pass on," Charles bitterly shared. "The aides were laughing about it. Dirty little snots."

"Well, pardner, we may be riding into the sunset soon," Laurel murmured sadly.

Laurel turned to Charles and patted him on the shoulder. "Thank you for being a good roommate," she said sincerely. "I still don't know why you are here."

Charles was deep in thought a moment, then sat up abruptly, pulling his knees up and drawing his blanket protectively around him.

"Let me tell you my story, and then maybe you will understand," he began.

"I was a loan officer at a large bank for nearly twenty-five years. You'd know the name if I told you. My wife Helen and I had no children, but we lived the high life. It was fine dining, golf on the weekends, cruises, trips abroad, you know the drill. After thirty-two years of marriage, it was pretty routine and comfortable for both of us."

"My wife was pretty spoiled. Well, pretty and spoiled you might say. She was an only child and had been pampered. I continued to pamper her. She had her bridge group, and hair appointments, charities, all the conversation she needed. For me, she was the perfect adornment at the events we had to attend."

"Of course, I was surrounded by clients who wanted my favor and attention, a staff that treated me well, and colleagues who were interesting and of the right sort. You know the kind."

"My personal family was small, just myself and an older sister, Esther. She was so much older, it was like I was a second family so we were never close."

Charles stopped and looked at Laurel. "Am I boring you?"

"No," she said, her eyes holding his, "Go on."

"Then, four years ago Helen got a glioblastoma brain tumor. She had trouble walking, her speech was affected and it quickly spread. It was terrible. She suffered, and I could do nothing to help. We spent thousands on treatment, but, well, she was gone."

"I had spent so much time with her, my job suffered and they "gave" me early retirement. My God, I was only sixty-three! I went into deep depression, unable to function. Our housekeeper got worried and called my sister to come see what should be done."

"Now my sister Esther had two successful marriages. By successful, I mean the men were rich and conveniently died at an appropriate age to leave her a wealthy, and selfish, woman."

"She had read about a woman of a certain age with no children, like us, who sold everything and moved into a hotel that had a restaurant attached. There she lived like a queen until her passing."

"Esther then read another article about a retired teacher who lived on a cruise ship, where there was not only food, but medical care! So she sold it all, except her classy clothes and jewelry, and booked a year-round suite on the Norwegian Cruise Line. It has been four years, and she rarely comes back to the Dallas area."

"When they called her to come see about me, her first reaction was dismay at my condition. Her next reaction was to put me in Meadowdale in assisted living. I became even more depressed, and they moved me upstairs, here to Windom Hall."

"As my Executor, with her shrewd business sense, the estate sale apparently was an excellent event. I will be able to stay here a very long time. Until Martin came along, I was content to stay in a grey fog, feeling sorry for myself."

"Now hearing you and Olive talk about what is going on, I have become curious about the financial mismanagement of this establishment. And about the malfeasance of the staff."

Laurel looked at him closely. "You seem different."

"I am, now," he asserted strongly, sitting up straighter. "I want to be involved in your little intrigue, to find out why Bobby got away with murder, what those nurses are doing to the patients, and the underbelly of the beast."

Charles turned to the side of the bed and sat up, stretched his legs tentatively.

"You know, laying about for so long has made me a bit weak. I think I'll start getting up at night and exercising, if it won't disturb Martin."

Laurel moved over to him and patted his shoulder.

"That sounds like a good plan. Get back in shape, get your body and your mind back on track. You'll feel so much better."

"I have been trained to detect fraud in the financial institutes, and I smell fraud here. Can I help?" Charles inquired eagerly.

"Charles, welcome to the Laurel and Harting team. Welcome to the world of the living."

Charles was living once more, but Death was on the move at Meadowdale.

CHAPTER 13

There was only one night aide to assist guests on Windom with their dinner. Charles took over the feeding of Martin, then went to the dining room to eat with Olive and Walter.

"Charles, I am worried that Martin will be moved soon. I heard Mykala telling Chantel that he is failing and needs to go to LaRonda. " Olive looked at him beseechingly. "What can we do?"

"I'm not sure. I've taken some of the weight off the staff, but I can't tip my hand totally or I may get booted out. I don't take the meds anymore. Actually I hide them under my tongue so they think I am taking them, and try to seem to be sleeping like I was before, but it is getting harder and harder to lay around and do nothing."

"Well, that Mykala is just a trouble maker," Olive announced loudly.

Calista came around the corner, a storm cloud on her face.

"Miss Olive, I am SURE that she is not the only trouble maker on this unit. Now, if you will march your little old self, and yes, I said OLD self, back to your room, I would appreciate it. And take that sneaky little OLD man with you. He pinched my backside this afternoon!"

Calista stood with her hands on her broad hips and glared at the three of them. Walter smiled sweetly at her, then winked in a wicked way.

"You are a dirty old man," Calista exclaimed.

"Well, I would be a clean old man if you would shower with me," suggested Walter.

Olive stood up, took Walter's arm and led him down the hall to their room. Walter looked over his shoulder and called, "I promise not to drop the soap again."

"Hush," giggled Olive.

Charles meandered slowly back to the room he shared with Martin. The DVD player had gone black. No one bothered to even restart the movies anymore.

The next day Sanjay Singh, the P.A., was sent to use the Visual Analogue Scale to rate Martin. It was the usual way to test geriatric patients with impairments due to strokes, Alzheimer's and Parkinson's since the patient himself could not describe their pain or reaction to medication.

Sanjay held Martin's hands and looked into his face. "Martin, how are you feeling today?"

"They wouldn't let me leave last night," Martin explained. "I tried to go home, but the police had my room under surveillance and I couldn't get out."

"I asked them to leave," Sanjay assured him. "Now, other than that, how do you feel?" Sanjay watched his face closely for signs of pain. Martin's right hand began to shake violently and his voice shook.

"Why can't I go home? What have I done?" His pitiful

gaze made Sanjay say gently, "Do you have pain, Martin? Do you hurt at all?"

"I am just so confused. No one comes to see me." The sadness touched Sanjay.

"Your wife was here yesterday, Martin."

"Really? Laurel was here? Why didn't someone come get me?"

Sanjay gave up. "On a scale of one to ten, how is your pain?"

"Maybe a five, or seven."

"What hurts? Where does it hurt?" Sanjay urged.

"My arm, where I hurt it when I fell."

"You fell?" Sanjay said sharply and pulled up the sleeve on Martin's left arm, which revealed a nasty bruise.

Charles rolled over and sat up. "He fell two days ago and hit his arm on the sink. Chantel said they ordered pain meds for him."

Sanjay went to the nurse's station. "I understand that Martin Baley has pain meds ordered. Can he have another one today?"

Yvonne looked up. "He can have as many as he wants. He just never asks for them."

Giving her a hard look, Sanjay said, "And did it occur to you that he is here because he does not know how to ask for pain meds? You need to check him, touch the wound and see if he winces."

"Don't they train you to use a pain thermometer to measure the pain, or to see levels of discomfort from their facial expressions? Most of these people don't have the capacity to just tell you how they are."

Yvonne just shrugged and went back to texting her friend.

A few days later, Joe Cirgenski shed his clothes in the dining room and began hollering that the Russians were coming. The nurse on duty immediately called for the aides to restrain him, but he overpowered them and headed for the garden.

"Call Dr. Punjab! Nurse Bernice! Nurse Bernice!" Betty Jane called as she ran after him.

By the time Dr. Punjab arrived, Joe was sobbing in his room, wrapped in a terry robe while aide Betty Jane held his hand. Dr. Punjab gave him an injection, and in a short time he was no longer shaking. Joe was asleep.

Alerted by Rani, Dr. Sanjay Singh came up to the wing to see what was happening.

"Dr Punjab, I checked the chart, and Mr. Cirgenski has been taking low doses of opiods for the pain in his sciatic nerve. I am wondering if this is causing the delusions and inappropriate behavior? It has been charted on several occasions."

Rani nodded her head in agreement. "He has been acting strange. It is difficult."

Dr. Punjab glared at them. "And when did you get your degree in medicine? Are you questioning my treatment?"

They looked at each other, then Dr. Singh said softly, "Rani, Miss Roshan, I will handle this."

She dropped her head in deference and moved down the hall.

"What do you suggest, Dr. Punjab?"

"I am giving him an anticonvulsive because I believe

he has had an episode of petite mal. His reaction is from coming out of the epileptic episode."

When Latesha Vernon, the night aide, made her late night rounds she found that the Grim Reaper had gathered another victim. Joe Cirgenski, in room 209, was finally healed of his earthly ailments.

CHAPTER 14

It was rumored that 209 was an unlucky room. First Albert Phillips, and now Joe Cirgenski was gone. Their roommate, Chester D'Wores was waiting for his next "friend". Soon enough, Paul Enmary was scheduled to be moved from Julep to a bed across from Chester's.

Haliburton Hall was getting a new resident also.

Olive was pleasantly surprised when a buxom woman with obviously dyed red hair (the grey roots in her center part gave her away) and her pudgy, black-haired husband toddled down the hall toward Room 207. From the elevator behind them came an aide wheeling two heavy suitcases as she struggled to the "singles" wing.

Olive hurried down to greet the newcomers. Another woman she could talk to, what a treat.

"Hi there, I'm Olive Harting. My husband and I are in 215. Welcome to the Memory Care Unit." Olive extended her hand, but the lady (who greatly resembled an older Bette Midler), gave her a hug.

"Hey, I'm Darlene Dooley, and this great big galoot is my husband, Richard. He is moving up from assisted living. Can't live with me, can't live without me."

Darlene noticed Olive looking at Richard's dark black

hair and quipped, "People are always saying, "Did someone dye?" and we say "Yes! We did!" She giggled girlishly and struck a pose.

"Getting old isn't for sissies, and we are going to do what we can to avoid looking like geezers." She slapped Richard on the bottom and said loudly, "Ain't that right, Ricky dear?"

He took a step back and looked at her suspiciously. Darlene just smiled lovingly up at him.

"Poor thing, half the time he doesn't know me. When I play like this, he doesn't know whether to flirt with a pretty stranger or be offended." Then she whispered, "And he is also going deaf, which has become a blessing of sorts."

Olive found her amusing and endearing, especially after being surrounded by men who didn't know what day it was.

"Were you both in Julep? Now that Richard is here, will you stay there?" Olive asked softly.

"No way kiddo! I plan on heading for an Independent apartment. Don't want to leave Meadowdale. Why look for new digs? When I'm a real old fogey they can just slide Richard over and we can have a two-fer." Darlene began digging into her voluminous red handbag. "Gotta get my smokes while Prissy gets Richard settled. Ta Ta!"

With a pack of Malboro's in hand, and a gold lighter, Darlene punched the code in the keypad by the elevator and headed downstairs to smoke.

Prissy came out of the room and acknowledged Olive.

"They are a cute couple, aren't they?" Prissy asked. "I'm glad Darlene has found a friend."

"I think she has," smiled Olive. Most of the women who came to visit their husbands exhibited such sad, hopeless faces that Olive avoided getting close.

A few days later Darlene and Richard joined Olive and Walter in Windom's dining area. Darlene preferred eating with her friends to the gloomy group in Haliburton's larger dining room.

"Boy, kiddo, this chow is terrible! Gummy spaghetti, peas and carrots, cold garlic bread and a dry brownie. Downstairs, the food is pretty good. I can even have a big salad if I want. What gives?" Darlene complained.

Olive smiled and replied, "Most of the men in Windom don't really know what they are eating. If they are needing a special diet, it usually doesn't happen. Those folks move on to the Last Roundup."

"Well, kiddo, you need to join me sometime when your sweetie is sleeping. I'll treat you to a good meal and bingo in the big dining room downstairs! It's a hoot."

Darlene shared that Tuesday and Thursday are Bingo days. Wednesday is a Sing-along, and Friday is Family Movie Night with popcorn.

"But Bingo on Tuesdays is the best. Their ball cage is old and defective and the caller is from some European country. Half the time he has to repeat the number two or three times. They are from the Church of the Perpetual Virgin, I think."

Olive snickered. "I've got to see that."

Olive watched in fascination as Richard unscrewed the cap on the salt and made a mound on the table. He then took his fork and made a squiggle. Walter took the cap off the pepper and poured into the salt. Richard looked up quizzically.

"Integration," explained Walter.

The two of them began "finger painting" in the spicy granules with their forks, sort of a Zen garden.

"I think we will get back to our room," said Olive, gently extricating Walter from the chair.

"See ya later kiddo," replied Darlene. Darlene, in her 3 inch stilettos, sauntered off with Richard walking stiffly like a zombie, to his room.

Carl, in a grey sweater, wandered into the dining area. He walked back and forth before he settled in a chair near them.

While Olive cleaned up the salt and pepper, Walter moved the forks into a pattern, tines north, then south. Olive smiled at his play.

Then she noticed Carl had pulled the yarn on his sweater, and a pile of crinkled wool on the floor beside him as his sweater lost row after row.

"Carl, I think we need to get you back to your room," Olive said softly. She took him by one arm, and took Walter by the hand as they went to room 210 across the hall.

Olive helped him off with his sweater and put his bathrobe on him. Carl frowned, but allowed her to dress him. She sat Carl in his chair and said, "I'll send someone for you."

As Walter and Olive started back to their own room, she noticed Calista going through the files at the Nurse's station and taking photos with her phone. Nurse Bernice was down the hall doing a special procedure on Chester D'Wores.

"I wonder what's up?" Olive thought. "Is she a spy? Is she working for Khan or the brothers, or for herself?"

Calista seemed to always be there when something happened.

Things are getting curiouser and curiouser.

CHAPTER 15

The curiosity about Calista was forgotten the next day when Darlene came clicking in on her bright red stilettos in a skin tight scarlet skirt with a flowing flowered blouse, her red hair flying out with electricity. (She looks like Bette Midler in that witches movie, thought Olive.)

"Hey girlfriend, how about Bingo tomorrow afternoon?" Darlene had a big grin on her face.

"Tomorrow is Tuesday, and that is the really fun one, right?" responded Olive.

"Yup, and you can bring Walter too. They never check. We will sneak on over and it will be a hoot!" Darlene chortled.

Charles was dressed in his green striped pajamas, but now he wore a loose fitting suit coat with them. Charles wandered over to their table. "What's for breakfast?"

"The same rubber eggs, limp bacon, cold dry toast and coffee you can watch a goldfish swim in," replied Olive.

"Yum," sighed Charles. "What are you two up to now?"

"Bingo!" they cried in unison. The other two residents in the room turned to look at them, then returned to their breakfast.

Charles looked sad. "I don't know if I can sneak out

with you. Unless there is an aide who doesn't know me, I can't leave my room. Fortunately today the staff is mostly part-timers."

"We'll work something out. How is Martin doing today?" Olive inquired.

"I think they are sedating him more and more. With the Parkinson's he has been delusional, which means he acts out. I am afraid it is the Last Roundup for him soon. I told Laurel and she was devastated."

Olive thought for a moment. "That must be why she has been avoiding me. If he goes up there, she won't have a reason to be here with us. This has become her life, and it will be hard to just sit and watch him sleep until they call hospice."

"Well, he hasn't gone yet, so let's see if we can help put off the inevitable." Charles said emphatically.

"Okay, so we'll plan on Bingo tomorrow. After lunch go back to your rooms as usual, and at 2:00 meet me at the elevator. I'll get you into the game," grinned Darlene. She really didn't know Martin and Laurel, and wanted to lighten up the atmosphere.

"Super," said Olive. They shared a conspiratorial grin. "Here's to tomorrow!"

When she got off work, Laurel went to sit with Martin. Charles sat up in bed and watched her sad face. Martin was dozing with an open mouth, his breath even, but labored.

"So, Laurel, I am afraid they are going to send him to the Last Roundup soon," Charles said softly.

"I know. The nurse discussed it with me already. If he isn't sedated, he gets agitated. If they do sedate him, he might end up with pneumonia. He doesn't even watch his movies anymore. I know he won't get better, but I'm not ready to give up," Laurel responded.

"I can put on the movies and pretend to watch them," Charles offered. "That way they will think he is still engaged in life. Maybe he will be more alert, and I can still act as if I hate it."

"Maybe Derreck can fly out and visit. Our son really connects with Martin. He just changed restaurants, but he should be able to get a Monday off," Laurel said excitedly. "Jewel has the kids to worry about, but I'll see if she can fly out too. And, Richard Gerard may come over before Martin is gone. I just want him to feel loved."

"That's the plan then," Charles said, relieved that action would be taken. The team would still be together for a little while.

"And what can we do about Calista?" he asked. "Which side is she on? And what else is going on with the illegalities? Are the brothers involved or is it just the administration?"

Laurel thought for a minute. "I can do some leg work. I'll go to the storage place Saturday morning, and also check into the Smith funeral home, as if I am doing a pre-needs. Let's see who is really involved. They say follow the money, and I have a feeling that there is a bundle of it somewhere."

"We really haven't talked much, and I can't leave my room after 6 o'clock without suspicion. These aides will figure out I've been pretending to be bed-bound," said Charles. "I get the feeling that Martin wasn't always a city boy, although he was a successful music publisher."

"Well, Martin grew up in Union Valley," Laurel began. "Those boys only dated Royse City or Greenville girls so they didn't accidently marry a cousin. I'm not joking. Those families were farm families and had been on the land for generations. A trip to Dallas was a real trip."

"Anyway, he and his cousin Don were a couple of scallywags. One time they had a fight in the barn, throwing seed at each other. Unfortunately mixing seed was a real crime, as his dad had no idea what he was planting that year."

"Martin was the class clown in High School, but because he was tall, he excelled at sports, and his personality was light-hearted and caring. Everyone liked him."

"He started in insurance, but music was his real love. One day a radio announcer complained their ad manager was an idiot and couldn't count worth a darn."

"Martin went to the station on his lunch hour, and the next day resigned from the insurance company. He never looked back. His business skills were apparent. He was likeable, could negotiate, and had a guileless air about him. His honesty was respected."

"One day, this was during payola, a music producer stopped in to hand out some new release, and after ten minutes of meeting Martin hired him to be his music publisher. He moved to Sherman Oaks to work for Sal, and that's when we met, at Mark Levin's law office."

"Sounds like a match made in heaven," laughed Charles.

"At least it was legal," Laurel responded.

"His parents still lived at Union Valley, and his dad was a real kick. Chester Baley was a true man of the fields. When Jewel was a little over three we left her with them while I was in the hospital birthing Derreck. It was winter, and the snow had fallen. Chester took Jewel out to see the little animals in the woods. You could see their tracks in the snow."

"Suddenly a bunny popped up and started loping across the snow. "Watch this" Chester said, and whistled loudly. The bunny stopped, dug down into the snow and disappeared. Chester quietly snuck over, pushed his arm down into the snow and pulled out the bunny by his ears."

"Want to take the bunny home for dinner?" he asked. Of course Jewel imaged that cute little bunny sitting in her highchair, bibbed and waiting for carrots. "Oh please, please!" she clapped her little hands. They went off the house with their catch.

"When they entered the kitchen, Chester started to hand the bunny to Mamma Ann, "Here is our supper!" Mamma Ann took one look at Jewel's face, now openly distressed, and said, "Get that critter out of the house. I have chicken and noodles for lunch."

Chester just shook his head and led Jewel back outside. "Well, I guess he can just hop on home to his family." "Oh thank you Papa," said Jewel, relieved. And the bunny was just as happy, I am sure."

They both had a good laugh at the misunderstanding. Laurel later found out that Mama Ann gave Chester a lecture about children and how different they saw things. However, Jewel never forgot about taking a bunny home to have supper with them.

"Well, time to head back to my apartment. I guess Martin will just continue to sleep tonight." She looked at him with affection.

"Good night, old sport. You've had a good ride. I'm glad I was your side kick."

Laurel leaned down and kissed him on his pale, shrunken cheek.

After she left, Charles put on an old Roy Rogers video and settled back into the recliner.

"This is for you, partner. I hope we can keep you from riding into the sunset a bit longer."

CHAPTER 16

That night Olive called to ask Laurel if she could babysit tomorrow from three to five.

"I know it is hard for you to get time off, but this is an emergency. Darlene is taking me to Bingo on the Indie, and I can't take Walter, and she can't take Richard. We thought we would park them with Martin and Charles to watch a movie, but Calista threw a fit," Olive explained. "The only solution is to have a sitter with them."

"When is the Bingo game?" Laurel sighed.

"At 3:00, before dinner. Some of the prizes are candy and stuff," Olive said.

Laurel thought a bit. "Okay, I'll move my dental appointment for teeth cleaning up a week. I think I can make them take me at 1:30, and that will give me an excuse to be out of the office for the afternoon."

"Super!" Olive cheered. "I can't wait to see this Bingo game. Darlene says it is a hoot!"

On Tuesday afternoon, at two forty-five, Laurel arrived in the Unit, with a bag of popcorn and four candy bars.

Martin was still asleep in his bed, snoring softly. Charles sat up.

"What is the matinee today?" he asked cheerfully.

"Laurel and Hardy in "Flying Deuces", where they join the French Foreign Legion. We have watched it a hundred times, but it is still funny how they do everything wrong and wreak havoc only to escape in a stolen plane."

"Ah, a laugh a minute I am sure," Charles commented wryly.

Olive and Darlene hurried in with Walter and Richard.

"Well, here are the boys. We've got to run."

Olive had on her usual tweed jacket and gold silk blouse, brown pants and pearls, but she added large tiger-eye earrings that made her look more dashing. Of course Darlene was in a flashy yellow and black checked top, a bit low in the front, and tight black trousers that complimented her black patent leather high heels.

They were giggling like school girls when they left.

Walter and Richard sat in the recliners. Laurel had brought a straight backed chair from the visitor's room, and Charles just pushed his pillows up a little higher. Laurel passed out the small bowls of popcorn and started the video. Soon they were laughing as Hardy tried to get them out of the scrapes which obliviously Laurel managed to create.

RoJean Tuvall cracked opened the door.

"What ch'all laughin' about in here?" she demanded.

"Just a funny video," responded Laurel.

Walter added, "This is Saturday at the movies, my dear. Would you like to join us? I think there is room here on my lap."

"You, Mr. Walter, am just a bit too fresh for me," grinned RoJean. "Just keep it down a bit, why don cha?" she said, and closed the door.

"I guess you aren't her type," Charles said dryly.

Laurel gathered the bowls and passed out the candy bars. The three men took them eagerly.

"I wonder if the ladies are enjoying their Bingo," mused Laurel.

This Bingo was like nothing either lady had ever seen.

The ladies from the Church of the Perpetual Virgin were all excited about the game, and had laid out a bevy of prizes, from denture cream to hair clips. It seemed to be a very poor congregation, with a big heart. There was one of the aforementioned denture cream, two packets of Tucks (for those with hemorrhoids), three packs of colored hair clips, four zip lock bags of cookies (Oreos), five Gold Bond hand cream, and a Partridge in a pear tree.

No, actually it was a big pink plastic Easter egg which held a fuzzy little yellow chick you wound up. It walked like a drunken sailor for about three inches. Of course, that was the prize everyone wanted.

The two men from the church set up the bingo cage on a round table at the front of the room, and proceeded to hand out a bingo card to each person who attended. The dining hall was half full, with about thirty residents waiting excitedly for the fun to begin.

Mr. Rotterdammen, the caller, carefully placed the large board with indentations in which to place the balls which had been called on the table. Mr. Garmenduffer, his assistant, made sure all the small plastic balls were ensconced within the faulty wire cage and began to turn the handle.

Olive noticed several of the people closest to the table had "grabbers" of the kind used to fetch things from the floor. She was a bit curious at first, but soon it became evident as to why they brought them.

As Mr. Garmenduffer spun the cage, balls spewed wildly through the wires, bouncing recklessly hither and thither. Grabbers plunged at their prey. At one point it was a dueling match between two of the men for a single ball.

The harried aide rushed about collecting the errant balls, giving them back to Mr. Garmenduffer, except for one, which she handed to Mr.Rotterdammen.

"B-9," he drolled in a heavy German accent.

Someone hollered, "What was that?"

"B-9, as in what you want your test to come back, Harvey," yelled George, a tall man with a flashy bow tie.

"G-76," called Mr.Rotterdammen, when another group of balls had been collected.

"Gee, I wish I were 76 again," quipped Myrtle, the woman with thick eyeglasses and tight grey bun.

And so it went, with balls flying, grabbers reaching and silly quips until all the prizes had found new homes.

Myrtle ended up with the yellow chicken. Harvey offered her five dollars for it, but she refused. She just kept winding it up and watching it totter around her table.

Myrtle gave the pink plastic egg to Sophie Feldstein. "Maybe you could paint this one and pretend it is your Faberge egg," she laughed.

Sophie scowled at Myrtle. "I never did find it, you know."

Darlene had won a pack of blue hair clips, which she immediately gave to Olive.

"Don't say I never gave ya anything, kiddo," she said. Just then the aides came out with brownies, carrot cake and decaf coffee for all the residents.

Mr. Rotterdammen and Mr. Garmenduffer gathered

their supplies while the church ladies went around the room hugging all the ladies and patting all the gentlemen on the shoulder.

"We hope you had fun. See you next week," they chirped.

Olive and Darlene returned to the Memory Care Unit, laughing over the antics at Bingo.

"Haven't had so much fun in ages," said Olive. "I enjoyed those lovely desserts."

Laurel was ready for them with two happy husbands who were anxious to have their dinner.

Martin had only moved a bit, and Laurel watched him nervously.

"Do you think he is okay, Charles?" she asked.

"I think you need to get your kids here soon," Charles responded. "I don't think we can keep him here much longer. If he goes to the Last Roundup, can I have the videos and the player? I will pay you for them. I have become quite fond of the Thin Man and Fred Astaire."

Laurel smiled. "I don't think Martin will mind. For the past week he hasn't been very aware of anything, and Walter and Richard would enjoy a matinee every now and again."

That night before Laurel left, she kissed Martin softly on the cheek. He turned his head slightly toward her, but his eyes were closed.

"Good night dear friend. Sleep well. I sure miss you Martin," she sighed and slowly left the room.

The next morning when Bebe came in to get Olive's laundry, she had news to tell.

"Missy Olive, I need to tell you, Tia Marie and Orlando

got married this weekend!" Bebe giggled a bit. "And her new job is really good. I tell you she isn't a bad girl."

"That is great Bebe. Did she ever get her last check from here?" Olive inquired.

"No, and that is very strange. She did a letter to say goodbye and give her address when she quit. Tia Marie say she gave it to Calista the week she left. I ask Tia Marie about why she quit." Bebe looked puzzled. "She say Calista told her that she was being fired for bad work, so to go to the new place. Calista told her to write a letter and give it to her, so she did. The new place hire her because of Calista."

"That is odd," agreed Olive. "But at least she has a good job and a good husband, two things for which to be grateful."

Bebe smiled brightly. "I think so too. And I grateful for you, Missy Olive."

Taking the small stack of dirty laundry, Bebe moved quietly out the door, leaving Olive deep in thought.

Was Calista good, or bad, friend or foe? It was hard to tell, but apparently there was more to this than met the eye. Olive would keep her own eyes open even more.

CHAPTER 17

The hydrangeas in the prayer garden were beginning to fade. The leaves of the slender sweet gum trees were tinged with red about the edges. Autumn was approaching. As always, the Master Gardeners had planted new fall flowers around the base of the statue of St. Francis of Assisi. Brilliant crimson mums and purple kale made a kaleidoscope of color.

Supported by his walker, Walter stood by the water feature wall, gazing at it with a beatific smile on his face. Olive stood uncomfortably on the uneven cobblestones, waiting for him to turn around. "Another trip around the sun," he said quietly. Then he turned and smiled at his long-time companion.

"How many more do you think we have in us, Olive old girl?" he questioned.

This was the most lucid he had been in weeks.

"Each day is a gift, a present. I guess that is why it is called the Present," she responded softly.

The two of them walked slowly back toward Windom Hall in Meadowdale Manor.

The sun had been up for nearly two hours when Rani

arrived early to give Martin a bed bath. He had not been able to get up for two days, and she was worried.

"I think I will call Dr. Singh," she told Charles. "Should I also call Mrs. Baley and let her know he isn't doing very well?"

"Laurel's son is arriving tomorrow from California. Call the doctor," he replied.

Rani knew Charles was no longer depressed and bedfast, but she allowed the little charade to continue because she liked him.They often talked briefly about her educational goals. He was very encouraging.

Rani left to get Dr. Singh, when RoJean passed by.

"You up and around Mista Gordon?" she inquired sharply.

"Is it time for a shower, or should I get dressed for work, Shalanda? I think I should take the bus home soon," he said, slurring his words a bit and looking around as if unfamiliar with the room.

"The name is RoJean," she corrected him. "And I'll be back in about ten minutes to take you to the shower." She just shook her head. Those crazy men! She hurried off down the hall.

Charles worried that he couldn't keep up the pretense much longer, but he wanted to be there for Martin, and Walter, and now, Richard.

Olive and Walter were passing by on their way back from the gardens. "How is Martin?" Olive asked.

"Not too good. I think Dr. Singh is going to come today. It looks like a transfer will happen soon," Charles said.

"Too bad for Laurel for sure," Olive murmured.

"Come dearie, let's get those tasty eggs before they

get cold," said Walter, and tugged at her arm. She smiled lovingly at him. "Yes dear, those tasty rubber eggs. What a delight."

Darlene came in just then, dragging Richard behind her. She pushed him into the recliner and turned on the video.

"I need to get my hair done kiddo, and I really can't handle Richard right now. Let's have a little John Wayne for my man, okay Charlie boy?" Darlene whirled around before he could answer and clicked down the hall, leaving a river of Jungle Gardenia in her wake.

Charles sat up and glared at the men. "Time to get well or I will really be depressed."

Just then Dr. Singh came in to look at Martin.

"You boys having fun with your old Western movies I see," he smiled.

Charles lay down with his face to the wall as Dr. Singh quietly began his examination of Martin.

"Charles," he said over his shoulder, "has there been any change? Is he still not sitting up or interacting?"

Charles turned over and sat up again. "I think they sedate him. He doesn't seem to be aware of anything anymore."

"I've looked at his records, and they are not charting the medications, but I can tell he has been given something. It is my belief, and I hope I am not sharing too much, but the staff wants him gone. There is a wealthy man whose family wants him here, and in a shared room. Right now we don't have an opening unless Martin moves up."

Charles looked at him sharply. "Then, when they move Martin, I get a new roommate? That will be awkward."

Dr. Singh moved to stand by Charles' bed and looked down at him with a grin. "Yes, Charles, and you will either have to get better, or worse. You can't keep pretending any longer."

Charles grinned back at him. "I think I would like to try some of that Bingo Olive and Darlene are playing. Do you think they can find me a room in the Independent section?"

"I would highly recommend it," said Dr. Singh. "Start packing."

CHAPTER 18

Charles got up the next day, donned his ill-fitting suit coat and sat out in his recliner. Soon Darlene came in to talk with him as he had requested.

"So what is Indie really like downstairs? Is it really independent? Is it interesting?" Charles was curious about his upcoming move.

"Well kiddo, it is tons better than this. Just a bunch of old farts trying to make the most of the time left them," Darlene laughed. "They offer activities, trips and things to keep our attention off the fact that we really are not that independent. It's a whole lot better than the Assisted at Julep. I figured if Richard had to be up here, then I'd stay close by. After he is gone, I'm not sure what I will do. I may even go get me an apartment in the real world."

Charles winced. "I don't have that luxury. My sister Esther has my power of attorney and she is not about to let me out of here. I am sure being able to play Bingo and converse with other intelligent adults is a far better situation than sitting up here in the Memory Care unit and pretending to be comatose. I think they will move Martin this week."

"How is that going?" Darlene inquired.

Charles frowned. "I was able to convince Dr. Singh

to order all sedation stop until Laurel's children could say goodbye. He agreed, so at least Martin is more aware today. He looks awful."

"Have you guys figured out what the problems are? What evil lurks in the hearts of men here at Meadowdale?"

Now Charles grinned. "I think we are getting closer. That sleazy aide, Amy, is stealing meds and selling them. I'm certain of that. And our illustrious administrator has several schemes going that are beyond the greed of the Markowitz brothers. He has a gambling habit and Patel is doing creative billing, according to Laurel."

"Darn it," Darlene complained, "If Martin goes to LaRonda, Laurel won't be here anymore and she's our contact with the outside."

"I don't know. I think Laurel and Olive are on the case and will remain on it until it is completed," Charles said with certainty.

"Well, I'm gonna go out and smoke one last one for tonight before I turn in. Can't get a gig like this one very often, where we get to be snoops," Darlene said. "I was feeling like we were doing something important."

'We are," Charles assured her.

Laurel's heart was warmed when Derreck arrived late that night and made a brief stop in his father's room. Martin was able to open his eyes and there was even a glint of recognition. Laurel sat on the edge of the bed as Derreck pulled a chair up and in animated tones told his father about the Sushi restaurant and his new position. Laurel beamed proudly at Derreck, while she held Martin's limp hand.

"Mom," Derreck said suddenly, "Call Jewel. Have her

say hi, or goodbye, to Dad. I think she needs to be part of this in some way."

Laurel got out her cell phone and made the call. It was after nine in Indiana, but Jewel answered quickly. "I was thinking about Dad all day," she admitted. "How is he doing?"

"Not too well. When they move him tomorrow, they will also call in hospice," softly Laurel replied.

"Then let me talk to him," insisted Jewel.

"He can't talk, but I'll hold the phone so he can hear you," Laurel said.

"Let me do this," urged Derreck, "And you go out and get some coffee."

As Derreck held the phone to his father's ear, Martin's eyebrows went up and a smile lit up his sunken features. He could hear his little girl's voice. Martin held out his hand as if to stroke the head of his little daughter.

Jewel talked about their only fishing trip, and about her sixteenth birthday, when Martin bought her a Vespa. She told him she loved him and it was time for him to relax and rest.

Derreck thanked her for giving permission to go. Then, he told his father, "Dad, I love you. Time for you to hang up the saddle. Grandpa Chester and Mama Ann are waiting for you."

Laurel came back in with her own coffee and another cup for Derreck. "Still take it black with one sugar?" she asked. He nodded, taking it from her.

"I'll meet you at the apartment," Derreck said. "Why don't you stay with Dad for a bit?"

Laurel sat on the edge of the bed, softly singing "I come

to the garden alone, while the dew is still on the roses...."
Martin's face soften into a restful expression. He opened his
pale, unseeing eyes for a minute, then closed them again
with a sigh.

At ten, she left for home.

At three-thirty the nurse on duty called to say Martin
Baley had suffered a major, fatal heart attack.

Laurel was strangely relieved that Martin would not
have to take that ride to the Last Roundup at Meadowdale
Manor. His final ride was to the Master's bunkhouse
with family and friends who had ridden into the sunset
before him.

"Take that, Death," Laurel said defiantly.

Things moved quickly after that.

Since Martin's body had been donated to medical
science so his brain could be autopsied for scientific research,
Laurel just had a memorial service.

Nurse Bernice arranged for Haliburton dining room to
be transformed two days later so Derreck could be there.
Flower arrangements and plants arrived from fraternity
brothers, former co-workers and friends from all over. Jewel
sent a large basket of gladiolas.

Associate Pastor Jeff Heismann of the Church of the
Perpetual Virgin led the short service. Chloe Garmenduffer
sang a sweet rendition of "I'll Fly Away". Richard Gerard
spoke about Martin's career, how his humble attitude,
honesty and hard work were recognized in the music
industry.

"It is a great loss," Gerard said solemnly. "We will all
miss him."

Richard, Derreck, Olive and Walter, Darlene and

Richard, Dr. Sanjay Singh, Rani Roshan and two ladies from Laurel's office were in attendance. There was no casket, just a large framed photo of Martin surrounded by the flowers at the front of the room.

That afternoon Charles P. Gordon began his transfer move to Independent Living. It was time to live again.

He did take with him one VCR player with monitor. The library of movies included Westerns, musicals, comedies, and a fuzzy black and white shot at the Grammy's where Martin Baley was interviewing his friend and client, J.J. Cale. Several other well known artists made cameo appearances.

If the angels run out of songs to sing, there are some good writers who have graduated to the clouds who can help them out.

CHAPTER 19

The move for Charles from Windom to the Independent living was not without problems. His bed frame arrived a day before his mattress and box springs were brought down, and his bureau had two drawers missing. They were located with his mattress. The box springs was slightly damaged (it slid down the stairs), but at least he only slept one night in his recliner.

In his closet Charles hung his few oversized clothes. Nothing fit, since Charles had lost so much weight in the past few years. It was time to buy new clothes, he thought. But how, and with what?

Charles went to the office to speak to Dalia, the administration secretary.

"What do I do for money, and how can I get some new clothes?" he asked her quietly.

Dalia checked the computer for his account, then she laughed. "Mr. Gordon, you've had a patient account here for quite awhile. Your sister has put in a large sum every month for you to use, and you haven't touched it. I would say you could buy whatever you want. I will send Tracy down to help you go on-line and order some things. Or, you two could go on the shuttle to Northpark and have some fun at Saxs 4th Avenue. What is your choice?"

Charles thought for a minute, then said, "Send Tracy and the shuttle. I would like to see what men wear today."

For the next four hours, Charles and Tracy went to the major department stores at Northpark, choosing a nice suit for special occasions, several Oxford shirts, Dockers and Khakis, deck shoes and several outfits suitable for a cruise or travel. They came home loaded with bags and boxes.

As he put away his new clothes, Charles was feeling more confident and empowered.

"My wife always did the shopping for me. This time I got what I wanted. I really am back to the land of the living," he said to Tracy.

"I appreciate being able to help you," Tracy said. "And I appreciate the big tip. My son needs cleats for his sports, and this really helps. Thank you, Mr. Gordon."

"Thank you, Tracy. This is the start of a new life for me."

The next day Darlene arrived to assist him with setting up housekeeping in his new digs, as she called them. Darlene grunted as she helped Charles move his grey lounger into place in front of the TV set. The room was cozy although it was a studio apartment.

This bathroom actually had a shower, unlike the shared bathroom on Windom Hall. Those had simply a sink and commode. All showers were accomplished with the help of an aide in the common shower. There was also a mini kitchenette, with one cabinet, a sink, under counter refrigerator and a microwave.

Laurel had brought him two plates, two cereal bowls, and silverware for four as a house-warming gift. Olive had offered two coffee cups with the Starbucks logo she had received last Christmas, and Darlene had added two champagne glasses from the WinStar Casino. Charles was "uptown," as Darlene declared.

He finally sat down at the small table. "So what is happening in Room 211?" Charles inquired.

Darlene sat down on one of the two square black stools at the small table.

"Well," she said with a grin, "according to Olive, they are in for it up there."

"Harold the Hat Man moved from the private rooms in Haliburton because his wife Rose is trying to economize with a shared room. AND, his roommate is going to be an old geezer with a trust fund."

"Here is the crazy part. There are two nieces and a nephew. They don't care about the old man, just want the money. Olive heard one of them saying the court appointed trustee insisted Old Uncle be in a private room. How they will manage that in a shared room I don't know."

Charles wished he had seen the drama. According to Calista, it was something to behold.

When she walked into the room the middle-aged twins, Corine and Carlene, had shoved Harold's large recliner in front of his bed and pulled the privacy curtain shut, dividing the room. They began wrestling Uncle Samuel's large armoire from the foot of the bed and put its back to the curtain, with the T.V. facing Samuel's bed.

"What in tarnation are you two doing?" Calista demanded, glaring at them.

"Giving Uncle Samuel some privacy," simpered Corine.

(She said it the British way, sounding more like Pre-va-cee.) "He needs a private room, after all."

"Is that right?" inquired Calista. "Then what are ya'll doing putting him in a shared room?"

"Well," said Carlene, "The Court Appointed Trustee insisted that when we admitted Uncle Samuel we were to put him in a private room. And WE are making this a private room."

"Yes, by pulling the curtain to the middle of the room, and placing the armoire in front of it, Uncle Samuel has his privacy," declared Corine.

The twins looked at each other and nodded in affirmation.

"Well, I never," declared Calista. She stuck her head out the door

"Mykala, get your tail in here. I guess we are doing moving duty today."

Mykala scurried in. The two large ladies pushed Samuel's green wingback chair into the corner at the foot of the bed, placed a night stand with a beautiful Tiffany lamp beside the automated hospital bed, then stood back to see their handiwork. Corine and Carlene watched a bit.

"I guess that will work," Corine admitted.

"Now, since this is a private room of sorts, make sure your Uncle Samuel doesn't infringe on Harold's Pre-va-cee. Always ask before you cross through his space to visit your uncle."

Corine giggled. "Oh, we won't be visiting. Carlene and I are the heirs. We are just making sure he is comfortable for his few, short, hopefully, last days."

Carlene smiled. "Well, there is one more heir, Neil

Armstrong. Not the astronaut, our cousin. Anyway, we three are the only ones who will be waiting," she corrected herself, "will be looking after his well being. And I doubt that Neil will ever come. They were never close."

Calista gave them the evil eye. "Humph."

She turned sharply and motioned to Mykala.

"Let's get Harold settled in. His wife is dining with him in the conservatory," she said in a hoity toidy voice, an obvious slap at Corine's airs.

They quickly pushed Harold's tall, narrow bookcase against the curtain to back up to the armoire, making firm the wall between the rooms. In the L-shaped corner left by the curtain and wall, on Harold's side, they placed his beige recliner with a goose neck floor lamp behind it for his reading. A generous end table was placed against the wall near the door, where he could place his books and nightly tea.

In defiance to the rules, they nailed a long hat rack to the wall for Harold's six hats.

The armoire had three massive drawers for clothes which Samuel would never wear. The T.V.'s remote was on the night stand. Samuel only watched science programs, so it lay untouched.

In contrast, Harold's plastic bin had three drawers. Rose rolled it into his closet beside the bed.

The beds flanked their closets, divided by a shared bath. Privacy was a joke, Harold and Samuel could look across the room at each other any time they wanted, which was never.

On Haliburton Hall Harold the Hat man was legendary. Every day he got up, put on a different hat (one for each day of the week, and the grey one twice for Sunday), picked up his newspaper (which had not changed in weeks), and strolled to the dining room by a big window.

There, in a nice easy chair, he settled in by the banana plant and streaming sunlight, to "read the paper." The aide brought a cup of tea, cream and two sugars, and he spent the next hour before breakfast pretending to read page after page.

There was a wing back chair in the same area, and sometimes his wife, Rose, would come sit with him and do her knitting. They rarely talked, just sat companionably, until he was through reading. "Breakfast," he would announce, and move to the table. Rose never ate at Meadowdale, but she was there daily.

What his memory issues were was unknown to the outsider. He sometimes had on nice slacks and a shirt, but often he still had on his blue pajamas. Margaret Ann, the daytime aide, explained to Dora, the afternoon replacement, that he had seven pairs of identical blue pajamas, which his wife kept laundered.

His was a regulated life. Well, it had been until Mrs. Rose Goldberg, his faithful wife, had been forced by financial constraints to move him to Windom Hall to a shared room.

That is when all the trouble began, according to Charles.

CHAPTER 20

A week later, Harold and Rose, Darlene and Richard, and Olive and Walter were all in the Windom dining area. They had pushed the two tables together to play UNO.

Actually, the ladies were trying to play UNO while the men were doing a wild version of crazy eights. They would add random cards and the ladies had to change their suit again and again.

Finally Richard made four walls and a room of his hand, while Walter did two teepees. The ladies gave up and just chatted.

"Where did you live when you and Harold met?" Darlene asked Rose.

"Oh, we lived in Chicago, in one of the buroughs. It was lovely. We had a little house, and Harold worked in the garment industry with a manufacturer. Finally we saved up enough to get a little shop, where he sold men's better clothing and hats, lovely hats. Harold adored hats and carried the finest, *and* a large selection."

"We were so happy. Our daughter, Anna, went to college, and met a man there who was a wonderful, loving man. Unfortunately, he wanted to go to Israel. They went there and lived in a kibbutz. She learned to speak Hebrew fluently. They had a son, Ari. We rarely saw them because it was so far to fly."

Olive asked, "How are they doing? Do they ever visit Harold?"

"Oh no," sadly Rose replied. "In 1989 there was a bombing on the bus, and Anna died, along with three other Jews. Ari was injured, but he is fine now. Saul remarried and they moved to Zurich where he works as a broker of sorts. We haven't seen Ari for years."

Olive turned to Darlene. "And what about you, dear?"

Darlene grinned. "My story won't make you sad for sure. I was raised in up-state New York, in West Seneca. In high school I played key board for a band, the Sexy Senecs we were called. It was a play on the word cynic, because we were all bored hippy types. Wild things back then, and full of piss and vinegar. Oh, excuse me Olive."

"No offense taken," Olive assured her.

"Anyway, it was at a concert similar to Woodstock that Richard and I met. He was so mellow, and fun. He still is, in a weird sort of way. He sees things so differently than most people. Very creative and out of the box, ya know. Losing his memory is not as hard to take. I'm sure he has a wonderful world of somewhere up in his mind."

"We never had kids. Both of us drank and smoked, both kinds, if you get my drift, and I just didn't want to take the chance of having a two-headed alien baby, like you read about in the rags at the store."

"There was a furniture store his uncle ran, so when he retired, Richard took it over. We lived above it in an amazing flat. I could change out the furniture each month, and Richard was close by. But, as the years went by the neighborhood changed, got real seedy, real mixed and when the auto factory closed, lots of homes went on the block."

"Fortunately for us, there was a fire. I was at a vacation house at the lake, had all my valuables with me, so although the place was a total loss, we were okay."

"I had an aunt in Dallas, and she told us it didn't snow much here, so we retired in Frisco."

Rose interjected, "We moved to Grand Prairie when our store flooded. One of my best friends goes to Temple there, and offered to let us live in the other side of her duplex. It worked out beautifully. I am still there, next door to Sophie. So very nice," she faded off.

Darlene looked interested.

"A flood, your business was ruined in a flood?"

"Yes," said Rose, nodding, "A flood wiped us out."

"How do you set a flood?" Darlene wanted to know. Olive gave her a stern look and she sat back quietly. (Obviously setting a fire and setting a flood were too different animals.)

"I think the men are ready for their naps," suggested Olive.

As they took their husbands to their various rooms, Olive pondered Darlene's remark. Some people make their own breaks, that's for sure.

As soon as Olive got Walter settled, she phoned Laurel and relayed the conversation.

Laurel laughed, "I wouldn't take it too seriously," she remarked. "Darlene is a card, and it may or may not be true that they burned their own place down. However, the fact that they had taken all their valuables to the vacation home gives one pause."

"And how are you dear?" Olive asked gently.

"Okay," Laurel replied. "I really need to get back up and visit you. I want to go to Bingo, and try the dining room with the GOOD food. I miss you all so much. Losing Martin was hard, but actually I lost him years ago when the Alzheimer's and Parkinson's robbed him of so much."

"You know, when I saw that man unravel his sweater, it struck me as a kind of metaphor. All these men were once whole and lovely. Then, a little at a time, they have begun to unravel. I think that is why I am here, to try and keep it from pulling apart all the way," Olive said with a sigh.

"Why don't you come on over," encouraged Olive. "We need to find a way to expose the those from the dark side. I think that means look into the drug store, funeral home and storage unit. Let's see what trouble we can cause."

A few days later, while Walter was dozing in front of the television, they held a meeting to catch up on events. Laurel was seated in one recliner while Olive, in a velvet lounging outfit and Charles, in his new blue polo shirt and neatly pleated khakis, perched on the edge of the bed.

"What DID happen with the drug store and funeral home?" Olive wanted to know. She could not leave the Memory Care ward, and the group didn't venture far from Meadowdale Manor.

Laurel paused, then began to summarize what she knew. It had been almost two weeks since Martin had passed, and she finally felt strong enough to talk about it.

CHAPTER 21

Amy's snitch had been on top of things. The morning after Martin died, Amy arrived at Meadowdale early to collect any medication she could find.

She dropped her Coach bag in her locker, and changed into her scrubs, then headed upstairs to the medicine cart. It only took her a few minutes to find three prescription bottles from the Pill Box with Martin Baley marked on them. She checked off the chart, "Disposed of properly", slipped the orange bottles into her pocket, and hurried back down to the employee lounge. After jamming the bottles into her purse, Amy clocked in and started her shift.

That afternoon she left a little early, jumped into her grey Hyundai and headed to the Pill Box.

Although Martin's brain was donated to science, his body was to be cremated. Laurel had taken the day off to make funeral arrangements.

After she had gone to the funeral home, Laurel got a call from Charles signaling the pill switch they had agreed on was completed. She headed for the Pill Box instead of home.

According to Laurel, she arrived just before Amy entered, still wearing her scrubs. Amy was shaking her hips as if she were making ice cream. She strolled up to the counter where the druggist, Mr. Rupert was waiting. He looked around quickly as if checking for customer. When he saw no one nearby, Mr. Rupert opened a drawer under the counter, positioning himself so the surveillance camera was on Amy.

Neither of them had seen Laurel come in when another lady entered, or seen her position herself behind the tall medical device display. She had taken out her cell phone and recorded the entire scene between the druggist and Amy.

However, she was not close enough to catch their conversation on film. The video had to be enough to prove Amy stealing drugs.

Mr. Rupert motioned for Amy to slide the pills over. Laurel saw her place three bottles on the counter and he quickly brushed them into the drawer and closed it.

"Hey, where is my money!" she demanded loudly.

"Hand me a bill," Laurel heard him say quietly.

Amy searched her purse, and finally pulled out a dollar bill. He smiled, and turned back so the camera would see him taking a bill to the register. He nodded broadly, "Yes, I can change that."

He opened the register, audibly counting out fifty-two dollars. Amy shrugged.

"Better than nothing," she mumbled. "I can get some weed to sell and still have a dime bag for me." Marijuana cost $300 an ounce and $10, a dime bag, only bought one joint, she thought.

"Well, then I'll see you tomorrow," he said loudly with a false smile.

She did not look happy, but took the cash and left. He looked back toward the camera and pulled a tally strip from the register, circled an amount and put the strip in the drawer.

Mrs. Perkins came around the round display of cosmetics where she had been choosing a lipstick, and approached the counter.

"Thank you, and come again," Mr. Rupert called after Amy as she strode out. "Oh, hello Mrs. Perkins. Your prescription is almost ready." Mr. Rupert went up the few steps to his work space and began to prepare Mrs. Perkins' order.

The tires on the grey Hyundai squealed as Amy sped away, and Laurel eased out of the door.

"What happened at the funeral home?" asked Olive.

"Obviously Mr. Khan had already called Mr. Nafie to let him know I would be coming. What he didn't know was my ForeThought insurance with RestHaven was transferrable. He could not pad the bill for the cremation, but he was polite about it."

"I'm sure Mr. Naife has encountered this twist before and would let Mr. Khan know not to look for a kickback. Martin's brain went to the facility that studies Alzheimer's and the cremation won't take place until they have two more on ice. Apparently they save money on fuel."

"So he isn't a crook then," Charles said.

"He is only an employee. Smith is the owner and the one pushing fancy funerals. I've talked to two other wives about it. Although he is a bit high, their insurance covered a really nice casket and funeral ceremony. They were satisfied with Smith."

Walter had been dozing in front of the television when he woke with a start. Olive laughed.

"What are you laughing 'bout now?" he asked.

"Oh, you've been being a pill," said Olive.

"Not really, unless it is Viagra," smirked Walter.

"Walter!" exclaimed Olive.

"Well, I have been a little blue today," he grinned.

"Speaking of Viagra," Charles said, "the bottle of Martin's heart medication became some old Viagra pills of Richard's that Darlene gave me. The psychotic ones, don't remember the name now, they were big and white, so I substituted Gas-X. I was going to put all those they gave me that I spit out into another pill bottle, but they looked pretty groady."

"So glad you didn't use them. Olive, when I gave you the extra pill bottle, how did you know when to switch them? I was worried you would do it too soon and Martin would actually take one of the weird ones."

"When I overheard the nurse tell an aide they were about to move him upstairs, I knew they would toss the old drugs. They use stronger sedatives in the Last Roundup. If he went up, Amy was sure to pull those bottles. We just didn't expect him to die that night."

"Anyway," Olive continued, "I had Walter distract the nurse by asking her some questions, and he was extremely effective. Pulling the bottles and refilling them was easy, but getting them back on the cart took some doing. Lucky for me, someone down the hall turned on the trouble light."

Charles said, "Too bad the thought of being moved was too much for Martin. I think that is what gave him his heart attack. At least we were able to give bogus meds for Amy to steal."

Laurel smiled. "That was pretty clever of you two. How did you know she would take them, Olive?"

"It is her M.O., her method. Every time there is a death or a move, somehow she knows and tries to get to the med cart before the aide who is in charge of it can go through the proper procedures."

"That morning she came in before her shift. I guess her network had let her know there had been a death. She looked around to make sure no one saw her, but I was in the shadows by the alcove, and she pocketed all three bottles. She marked something on the clipboard. Later, she left early with that big Coach bag of hers smiling like a Cheshire cat."

"And THAT," spoke up Charles," is the reason Miss Amy is no longer here."

Laurel smiled. "Nurse Betty was very perturbed when I showed her my video. I told her I had just gone in to get some hairspray, when I saw Amy come in. I told her I took the video because I was suspicious from some talk on the grapevine. She watched it, and then had me go to Mr. Khan and show him. The rest is history."

"I wonder if the druggist is reusing those medications to fill other orders," mused Olive. "That is a nasty thought. Imagine the money he is saving, and the poor patient at Meadowdale that is getting recycled drugs." Olive grimaced.

Walter got up and took Olive's arm. "Let's go get a drinkie," he said pathetically. "It is MY turn with my Olive," he said, glaring at Charles and Laurel.

"Yes it is," agreed Charles. "I'm heading back to my room. It is Bingo night and Darlene and I got some grabbers so we will be part of the fun. Do you want to join us?" he asked Laurel.

"No, I've got to get back to the apartment. I got a letter about a class reunion and I need to make a decision about whether I want to go. I hate to go without an escort," Laurel said.

She got up, smoothing her pleated skirt and picking up her purse, she stooped to hug Olive.

"Well, we are just glad you still come to visit," said Olive. She walked Laurel and Charles to the elevator, hugging them both as the elevator door slid open.

As they left, Olive thought, life will be easier for Laurel now.

Easier perhaps, but Laurel's life was about to get more interesting.

CHAPTER 22

Darlene met Charles at the elevator. She had been out for a smoke again and overheard some interesting tidbits from some aides on the first floor. Apparently Mr. Khan had hit the jackpot again at the Casino and was flashing a Rolex. His secretary was furious because he refused to give her a raise after that. And, to top it off, his wife left him a few weeks before and it was just now getting out.

She couldn't wait to tell the others.

"How did it go?" she asked Charles, eagerly.

"Laurel filled us in on what happened at the Pill Box and the funeral home. We still don't know how they are scamming the families with the storage unit."

"Are you sure it is a scam?" asked Darlene.

"Everything else the Markowitz brothers are holding seems to be," replied Charles.

"In fact, there are things going on that have me really curious. I was behind the parrot cage last week, not really hiding, but Calista came down and slipped into Khan's office while he was out at a meeting."

"She photographed some files, and then accessed his computer and ran off something and left. I can't decide if she is a friend or foe," Charles mused.

"At this point, I don't care, kiddo, I'm ready for some hot Bingo. Let's go have some fun with Heiseman and Dinglehoffer." She had already forgotten her juicy tidbits of gossip.

"That's not their names," chided Charles with a grin as they went into the dining room where everyone was crowding as close to the caller as possible.

Mr. Rotterdammen had already placed the call board and Mr. Garmenduffer, was spinning the wheel. A ball landed at Darlene's feet, which she neatly snatched with her new grabber and held it aloft. Two other balls had been caught by seniors, but Darlene got her prize to Mr. Rotterdammen first.

"B-4," he intoned.

"Or after," laughed George Olson, adjusting his bow tie as he cracked up at his own humor.

Things went downhill from there, with Darlene winning a pen from Texas First Bank, and a notepad from the Boys Ranch inscribed "Mrs. Cloris Packman". Charles did much better, winning two koozies from KGVL, Greenville Texas. He had wanted the five dollar coupon to Wendy's but Myrtle, the lady with the thick glasses, won that.

Those sweet ladies from The Church of the Perpetual Virgin had been scounging prizes again, he thought. Well, he would sneak the koozies back into their bag before they left.

Charles and Darlene went back to their respective rooms in Independent Living. It had been a fun-filled evening after all.

Olive and Walter were sitting quietly in the visitors

lounge when they overheard Nurse Bernice talking with Calista.

"I should have seen it coming with that tramp, Amy," Nurse Bernice complained. "She only came in early to work when there had been a death or transfer. What a little sneak."

"How did they catch her?" Calista asked.

"It was that Laurel Baley," whispered Nurse Bernice conspiritorially. "She saw Amy at the Pill Box and got suspicious, so she filmed her with her phone talking with the druggist. Then she showed it to Mr. Khan."

"Wow, that was pretty clever of her," admitted Calista. "I heard rumors Amy was making money on the side, but I wasn't sure how she was doin' it."

"Well," went on Nurse Bernice, "Mr. Khan went to Mr. Rupert, who claims it was the part-time guy, Alvin McNabb, who was in on it with her. Rupert fired him when he found out. Khan confronted Rupert about the video. Mr. Rupert showed him the surveillance tape from the Pharmacy. It seemed to match what Mrs. Baley claimed was happening."

"Rupert said Amy came in pretending to want change, so he gave it to her. But, and this is the kicker, she was really bitchy about it. Apparently she was hoping McNabb would be there and she could sell him our patient's drugs!"

"When Mr. Khan questioned him about missing drugs, Rupert searched the drawer and found three of Martin Baley's pill bottles. They turned out to be filled with phony pills, so Amy was pulling a fast one on McNabb as well."

"Good riddance, I say," Calista said emphatically.

Nurse Bernice nodded her head in agreement. "The rule has always been no one touches the med cart but the assigned aide. On our shift, that's Kris Cross, the new girl."

"Makes sense to me," agreed Calista. She gave a sigh. "Better start my final rounds tonight."

As she walked past the visitors lounge, she looked straight ahead, seeming to deliberately avoid noticing Olive and Walter.

Friend or foe, that is the question.

The other question was, what would Laurel do about her class reunion?

CHAPTER 23

That was answered handily by Laurel the next day.

She had struggled with the idea of going alone, or trying to find an escort.

Laurel thought about asking Charles, but checking him in and out of Meadowdale seemed a bit of a challenge, since the party was at the Filter Building on White Rock Lake in Dallas. They would be getting back very late, so it didn't seem practical.

Anyway, she wanted an escort who would make her former classmates a bit jealous.

Laurel got out the phone directory and looked up "Escort Services" in the yellow pages. As she ran her finger down the page, she stopped at O'Malley's Escort Service. It sounded like a good Irish name, and she had a weakness for the Irish.

She punched in the number with some trepidation.

"Is this really an escort service?" she asked nervously.

"Yes mam," the girl on the other end replied. "When do you need an escort, and how far will you be traveling?"

"It will be next Friday, for about four hours. It is less than thirty miles one way. You provide the transportation?"

"Of course," said the girl. "I have Ramon, who is one of

our best. He is very reliable, and gets repeat customers. May I give him your number and you can firm up the details with him? We take Visa, MasterCard and Diner's. He will give you an estimate, but we expect payment at the completion of the transaction."

"I understand," Laurel said. She hung up with a smile. Then she frowned. She had not asked about the cost or any details.

Oh well, Ramon would call and they could make the arrangements at that time.

It was Wednesday when Ramon got back to her. Work had been hectic, and Laurel had not been sleeping well since Martin passed. Laurel had put off making hard decisions until after her class reunion. There was still some hope that she might run into Alex Carson, an old flame from her Junior year. A dream, only a dream, but where there is hope, there is life.

"Mrs. Baley," Ramon asked, "You called for an escort?"

"Oh yes. Is this Ramon?" Her voice could not contain her excitement.

"Yes it is," he said firmly. "You requested an escort for four hours, thirty miles one way. Now, I have to charge you for travel time and mileage as well, is that okay with you?"

Her mind drew a man resembling Ricardo Montalba from his Latin accent. That would be wonderful, a distinguished, handsome man on her arm.

"And what is your hourly rate," she inquired, holding her breath for the answer.

"It is seventy-five dollars an hour plus two dollars a mile, and one hundred dollars travel time to and from the job site. You only require one escort?" he asked.

She was a bit confused. "Of course, that is all I need."

"Where will I do the pickup?" Ramon asked, very businesslike.

Laurel took a deep breath. "531 Hopkins Street, Apartment J, in Garland."

"An apartment? That is unusual. Do you have all the paperwork in order, all the permits? Where is the final location?

"It is 2810 White Rock Lake in Dallas. I sent in the paperwork. I guess my permit is up-to-date, and, uh, what else was it?" she stammered. Was that her auto permit? Were they using her car or his? Laurel was perplexed, but she continued gamely.

"It is for an event, just this one evening. And just those four hours." She gave a deep sigh and blundered on.

"I really need an escort. My husband died two, well, nearly three weeks ago, and I can't do this alone."

Ramon replied reassuringly. "I do this all the time. I can handle it. Will you be following in your car?"

She bit her lip. "I thought you provided the transportation."

"No, we just do the escort service."

"I see," she said. "Yes, I have a car."

"Good," he said. "Let's see, we have a five hundred dollar minimum. You fall a bit under that, but I have to charge you the full five hundred. We will settle up at the site."

"Okay," she said. "Now, I need you here at five pm on next Friday."

Ramon seemed a bit flummoxed. "I don't think it will take four hours."

"But I NEED you for four hours," said Laurel firmly.

"It's your money," Ramon said, and hung up.

Laurel took the day off on Friday and had her hair and nails done at Curl Up and Dye down the street. Hurrying home, she slipped into a red dress with a gathered skirt that would be great for dancing. Her makeup done, she sat at the dining room table, nervously watching at the clock.

At promptly five o'clock the doorbell rang.

Laurel opened the door to find Ramon (it had to be Ramon) in grey coveralls with the blue logo "O'Malley's Escort Service." Just beyond him, on the street, she could see the large white pickup with the same logo. It had a ten foot pole mounted in the bed of the pickup, and flashing lights on the top of the cab.

"Where is the vehicle I will be escorting? Is it a mobile home or an event truck?" Ramon inquired, looking at her attire with curiosity.

"Uh, it is me. I want you to escort me to my class reunion." Laurel said, her brown eyes large with the knowledge that her plans were falling apart like autumn leaves off a dying tree.

The light was also dawning in Ramon's eyes. "Oh, well, we are not that kind of escort service."

"So I see," nodded Laurel, her eyes reflecting her dismay.

"Now I understand your response to my questions. I was busy fielding two calls, so I did not get as precise as I usually am," he apologized.

"I guess I don't get to go," Laurel sadly said. "How much do I owe you for the trip out here?"

"Wait a minute," Ramon said suddenly. "Just wait right here."

He dashed off to the truck and came back with a gym bag. Laurel eyed him suspiciously.

"What's that?" she said, cautiously.

"This is my gym bag. Oh, I go to this Salsa club on Friday and Saturday nights with my friend Jorge. With my very good friend Jorge, if you understand."

Laurel relaxed. "I think I do. And do you have your Salsa clothes in that bag?"

"I sure do, and I would like to escort you, the proper way," Ramon said, with a smile.

"The bathroom is right there," she said. "We can take my car, if you don't mind."

Ramon and Laurel made a grand entrance at six o'clock at the Filter Building, to the envy of all her old friends. Ramon was handsome in his white silk shirt and tight black pants and patent leather shoes. He flirted with Laurel shamelessly (all in good fun) and she laughed and danced with her cares forgotten for one short night.

Her silky brown hair was shining in her upsweep, and the red dress was perfect for dancing. She looked younger than most of her other classmates, especially with her young, fit escort.

Alex Carson, her old flame, was now balding and quite overweight. He was there with his third wife, a brassy blond with a big chest. Alex had been a successful builder at one time, but lost much during the last downturn. Now he taught computer science at Forney High School.

At ten o'clock, Ramon told Laurel it was time to leave. She hugged a few friends, exchanged business cards to "catch up later," and headed out.

When they got back to the apartment, Ramon said

sadly, "I will need to get your credit card for the five hundred dollars. I won't have to tell my boss what was transported as long as I turn in payment."

Laurel smiled brightly. "It is worth every penny"

That night, for the first time in a long time, Laurel laid her head on her pillow and slept soundly with a smile on her face.

CHAPTER 24

Laurel Baley waited patiently outside the door of Courtroom " B" at Garland Municipal Court. She had drawn Judge Maynor N. Fraxtion. In Courtroom "A" Judge Dewey Cheatem was holding court. A young man exited with a smile on his face and a notarized order in his hand.

"Jack? Jack Smith?" Laurel asked.

The man turned quickly, then, with an embarrassed look said, "No mam. I am Nicholas D'Wores."

"Sorry," she said. "You looked just like someone I know."

"Not very well, obviously," he retorted smugly, and strode out.

Laurel approached the clerk at the desk.

"Was that Jack Smith, of Smith Funeral Home?" she inquired.

The clerk looked on her notes. "Nope. That was Nicholas D'Wores, nephew of Chester D'Wores who died intestate."

"Chester D'Wores who was at Meadowdale?"

"That's right. Now, if you'll excuse me," the clerk dismissed her and turned back to her paperwork.

Soon Laurel was called in for the probate hearing. It was settled quickly, and she returned to work at the Law Firm.

At her computer, Laurel looked up Smith Funeral Home

again. Sure enough, Mr. Mercedes O'Riley Smith was the owner, along with his three sons, Jack R. Smith, Hannibal L. Smith, and Jason Smith. Mr. Naife was obviously only an employee and not an owner.

When she researched the LLC, she discovered that Dr. Patel and Mr. Khan were also on the board of the Corporation. Laurel searched the names for other entities, and discovered that Smith, Patel and Khan were co-owners of Rest Assured, which handled the estates of quite a few Meadowdale clients. When Laurel went to the web site, it was just as she suspected. Jack Smith was a dead ringer for Nicholas D'Wores.

It was time to call a meeting.

Laurel called Olive first. "We need to get together tonight to talk. See if Rose will watch the boys while we meet in the downstairs dining room."

"Okay," Olive said. "Glad to have you back. I guess Laurel and Harting are on the case again!"

"That's right, and I have some interesting news."

Olive went down the hall to talk to Rose.

"Can you take care of Richard and Walter along with your sweet Harold for an hour tonight? Laurel is coming to visit, and I really want to see her," Olive wheedled.

Rose smiled. "I have the game of LIFE, it is so much fun. I've been wanting to play it, so I think we can keep busy while you visit with your friend."

Olive gave Rose a hug and hurried to the phone.

"Charles? Laurel is coming at seven o'clock tonight and wants to meet with us in the dining room on Indie. Tell Darlene. Rose is going to watch the boys."

When Charles agreed, Olive hurried to arrange with the

aides to have a table for four ready in the visitor's room for Rose and the boys.

Laurel arrived downstairs promptly at seven with a briefcase, and the four of them went to a table in the back of the dining room. Charles got coffee for all of them and before they settled down to hear what Laurel had discovered, each one hugged her.

"We were afraid you were done with us," Charles said shyly, looking down as he adjusting the cuffs on his new Brooks Brothers shirt.

"And, kiddo, we have stuff to tell you too!" exclaimed Darlene. She took out a flask from her pocket and doctored her coffee. "Just a little something to keep me focused," she explained.

"Before you start, let me tell you what I heard a couple of days ago, kiddos." Darlene said breathlessly. "I was out for a smoke before I was gonna meet Charlie here for bingo. The aides were gabbing. Anyway, Khan's secretary, Dalia, was upset because he hit it big at the Casino again and wouldn't even consider giving her a raise! He spent it on a Rolex, and his wife got angry and left him."

They all took it in, mentally adding it to the list of clues they were gathering.

Olive took control of the meeting, nodding at Laurel. "It isn't the same without you, Laurel, but I am glad you are able to have your life back."

"Well, yes and no. The more I find out, the more I see we are on to something big." Laurel dealt out the packets to the crew. "Let's take a look at what we have so far."

While Laurel spread out her chart, things were lively up on Windom Hall.

Rose was handing out the little cars and people for the game of LIFE. Richard was spinning the wheel again and again, while Walter lined up the little pink and blue sticks that represented the boys and girls. Harold took all the cars and lined them up.

"WAR!" Harold the Hat cried and flung a red car at Walter. As he was rearing back to hurl a yellow car at Richard, Rose took his arm and said, "How about some ice cream, Harold dear?"

Immediately he put the car down and stood up. "Ice cream? YEAH!" Harold pulled his tan Fedora down further on his head and stood at attention.

Walter's eyes brightened as he and Richard stood up too, the game forgotten.

"Ice cream?" both the men asked eagerly.

"Yes," Rose said firmly. "Time for ice cream. Mykala, may we have four of those vanilla ice cream cups?"

"You bet, Miss Rose," Mykala said, who was slowly picking up the game pieces. "I'll get it right now. Why don't ya'll just go sit in Walter's room and I'll bring it in there."

The four trooped into Walter and Olive's room. Harold and Richard took the recliners while Walter perched on his bed. Rose pulled the small side chair from Olive's side of the curtain.

After she had turned on the television, Rose made sure each man was comfortable and then looked out the door for Mykala.

The aide had a tray with four cups of ice cream, plastic spoons, and four small cans of apple juice.

The game of LIFE forgotten completely. Soon the men

were laughing at "Funniest Home Videos," and spooning up the cool vanilla treat.

The laughter in the Memory Care Unit was healing, but there was no laughter where the other four friends were pouring over the paperwork Laurel had brought them.

CHAPTER 25

Charles looked at the paperwork in front of him.

"I knew Patel was overbilling the Medicare accounts. I think Calista was checking that out too. It appears those guests who have no family and sign up to Rest Assured receive their EOBs, uh, the Explanation of Benefits, at Meadowdale."

"Apparently those letters are just filed away and probably shredded annually to avoid postal fraud. Since no one sees them, the overbilling isn't even noticed," Charles explained.

"However, I think there is some kind of audit going on. Mr. Khan has been meeting with Patel frequently in the last two weeks. This is serious business." Charles held up the Rest Assured contract that Laurel had copied from Mr. Simon Phillips' file at the Infirmary.

"Obviously Carol got whatever was coming to her, or maybe at that point she didn't care, but it looks like this group was not created for the benefit of the client," Laurel agreed.

"I discovered that if there is no next of kin, Rest Assured would go to Judge Dewey Cheatem, who would make someone on their board the executor of the estate with Power of Attorney, or appoint them as the Court Advocate.

I saw Jack Smith pose as a nephew for Chester D'Wores, who passed a couple of weeks ago. That way they get to keep siphoning off the money from the estate."

"What a bunch of crooks!" exclaimed Darlene.

"Are the Markowitz brothers in on this?" Olive asked. "I know you can't go to Mr. Khan again, because it is obvious he is part of the swindle."

"He absolutely is a part of it. Probably the head of it!" Laurel said vehemently. "Khan got his position from a recommendation from Dr. Patel. They are both partners in Rest Assured, and are involved with Smith Funeral Home. They also get kickbacks from the Pill Box, because they placed Mr. Vincent Rupert as the head Pharmacist."

"So how are the Markowitz boys involved?" asked Olive again.

"I don't know if they are involved in the swindles, or are just good businessmen. I've looked into their background and it seems pretty straight forward."

"The family came from New York diamond sellers, you know, Jewish immigrants. In 1983 the grandfather, Thomas Markowitz, Jr., opened a jewelry store in Houston. He shortened his name to Marko and was a great success for many years."

'I contacted Randy, my firm's private investigator. He found out that Saul and Abe also worked at the store. Abe became a gemologist, but it really wasn't his heart. He had a business degree and he wanted to make his mark his own way."

"When His grandmother required a nursing home, none were really where the brothers wanted to place her. In 1986, oil and gas had started to tank, so the brothers thought "baby boomers" and bought into the Pineview Retirement Community in Houston for grandma."

"According to the records, that is when they started to diversify and add a Pill Box Pharmacy and Load and Lock Storage in each town where they purchased a property."

"After Pineview, Shadow Mountain Retirement Community in Austin was next, and then in early 1995 they purchased Meadowdale Manor here."

"The brothers still live in Houston. Their Corporation holds the drug stores and storage as an investment. They have no funeral parlors in Houston or Austin, so I think Smith's is Khan's brain child. From what I can tell, the brothers aren't involved with Smith's or Rest Assured," Laurel explained.

Olive looked concerned. "How does this affect our loved ones?"

"There are so many things that are not kosher. I mean, the druggist is probably repackaging the pills from Amy and selling them back to Meadowdale. Patel seems to be overmedicating those in LaRonda. Also, one of the aides said they move people from Memory Care to LaRonda if they need a room for someone from assisted living. That is so wrong," Laurel fumed.

"And if there is fraud involved, the place may be closed down!" declared Charles.

"How do we tell the brothers?" asked Olive, getting right to the point.

Darlene said, "We need proof, real proof. And we can't count on Khan or Patel to help with that!"

Laurel thought for a minute. "Give me a week, and we will meet again."

"And we will see what we can discover here," Charles said. "Darlene and I are here near the office. Maybe we can find something in the trash, or accidently go in there when Khan was out and his secretary is away from the desk and snoop."

"Just don't get caught. Now, it's time for Olive to get back to Walter. I am sure Rose needs to get Harold to bed." Laurel hugged each one, giving Olive an extra tight squeeze.

After she left, Charles said, "You ladies are something else. This may get messy, even dangerous. Are you ready?"

"Hide and watch," Darlene said firmly.

"I'm ready," agreed Olive.

They did not realize how dangerous it could become.

CHAPTER 26

Neil Armstrong and his "girlfriend" Sheila Bunachellie got out of the elevator. His arm was tight around her waist and her head was thrown back in laughter, the mane of golden hair flowing wildly. She was the image of Carrie Bradshaw at about fifty, if Carrie (of Sex and the City) had been ridden hard and put away wet.

They headed to the nurse's desk. Neil leaned over to sign the visitor's book, then asked Nurse Yvonne Gutierrez, "Hey, where is Uncle Sam?"

She looked at him sharply. "To whom are you referring? And, who are you?"

He grinned a boyish smirk, "Neil Armstrong, and my Uncle Samuel Prescott is in here somewhere."

She sighed. "Room 211," Nurse Gutierrez said, and pointed down the hall.

The pair went down the hall, hips bumping.

"Don't disturb Mr. Harold," the nurse called after them. Too late, their laughter swept down the hall as they turned into Room 211.

Neil and Sheila pushed past Rose, who had moved to the door to see what the commotion was. "Where is the old man?" Neil asked.

"Your uncle is there," pointed Rose to the curtained area. "In his private room."

"Private room? Are you kidding?" Sheila said querulously.

Rose smiled sweetly. "It is private according to Corine and Carlene."

Sheila swished past Rose and Neil and went over to Samuel's bed. He glared up at her, but Sheila spread herself across him and nuzzled his ear. "You dear old man. Neil has told me all about you. How you are such a great scientist and SO smart."

She cuddled closer as Samuel raised his head a bit and eyed her suspiciously.

Sheila breathed into his ear, "I think you are amazing and SO cute."

Neil went behind the curtain and pulled it shut, blocking Rose and Harold from view.

"Okay Sheila, work your magic," Neil urged.

"How would you like a massage," Sheila purred, her hand wandering down his chest and pushing back the covers.

"Uh, mmghf, chhhm," mumbled Samuel, whose mouth had gone dry. He motioned for paper and pencil. Neil found them on the side table and handed them to the elderly man who struggled to sit up. He wrote something and placed it on his crotch. "KEEP OUT!" it read.

Sheila sat up and glared at Neil. "Well, I NEVER!"

"And you never will," croaked the old man. "Get out. GET OUT!"

"Is everything okay?" called Rose.

"We were just leaving," muttered Neil, as he pulled back

the curtain. He and Sheila hurried out, no long cuddling as Neil quickly signed them out and they boarded the elevator.

When they got to the parking lot, Neil turned on her.

"This partnership depends on you either seducing the old man, or helping me kill him in a way they don't blame us. Obviously seduction isn't going to work."

"Oh drop it," she said, dismissively. "He is almost gone now."

"So how did you get rid of the last two husbands?" he asked. "We need to go to plan B."

"I'll give you a milk shake for him tomorrow. Don't drink it yourself, and you'll have to go it alone. He doesn't seem attracted to me, or maybe to any woman." Sheila caressed Neil's cheek. "And doll, this is a financial arrangement only. Don't get any ideas."

Neil looked at her sharply. In the harsh daylight the liquid makeup had creased in the wrinkles of her forehead and the wattle of her neck was more of a focus than her large breasts.

"We agreed on a price, and once he is gone, and I get my part of the estate, you will be able to get all the plastic surgery you need to hook another big fish."

"Gee thanks," she laughed. "I've still got it, and there are plenty of guys over seventy that would love to get it too."

They got into Neil's silver Lexus and drove out of the parking facility.

The next day Neil was back again. This time without Sheila.

He strolled down the hall to Room 211 with a big chocolate shake and a bendable straw. He was grinning as he passed the nurses' station. He gave Nurse Bernice a nod.

Calista came out of Major Astor's room as she saw him enter Room 211 with the milkshake. Her brow furrowed with concern, but she didn't have to worry.

As he walked in, Rose stopped him.

"What have you got young man?" she demanded.

"Why, a yummy chocolate shake for my dear Uncle Sam," he said brightly.

"Oh no you don't!" Rose declared. "Your Uncle Samuel is a diabetic and he cannot have that sugary treat without a nurse approving it."

"Oh lighten up," Neil frowned, "If I want to treat Uncle Sam, it's my business, not yours."

Calista came in. "I'll take that," she said, holding out her hand.

Neil acted as if he was handing it to her, but fumbled and spilled it on the floor.

"Oh drat," Neil apologized insincerely. "Sorry about that."

He put the cup in the trash. "Guess you can clean it up while I visit with my uncle."

Neil went into Samuel's room and pulled the curtain.

"Okay Uncle, this is Neil. I know I haven't been very close to you before, but the girls seem to have abandoned you, so it is up to me to make sure you have everything you need while you are here." He patted his uncle's hand, fluffed his pillow, and smiled once more before he exited the "private room". Samuel gave him the fish eye and turned his back for emphasis.

When he left, Calista fished the cup from the trash and scooped some chocolate liquid from the floor back into it.

"I think I'll send this to be tested," she told Rose. "I don't trust that young man."

Rose shook her head. "I am just glad you came in."

After Neil signed out in the visitor log he headed for his car, where he called Sheila. "He is a diabetic, so they wouldn't let me give him the milk shake."

"So what did you do with it?" Sheila asked.

"Spilled it on the floor and tossed the cup," Neil said confidently. "It is cool."

"Good job," Sheila said and hung up.

Neil sat in the car and thought for a few minutes, then drove to Mockingbird to an exotic pet store.

There were no doggies in the window, or goldfish, but they did advertise "piranhas, boa constrictors and scorpions". Neil parked and walked in.

CHAPTER 27

As Neil walked out of "Pete's Precious Poison Pets" he had two bags. The smaller one was buzzing ominously. It contained the two flies, free with purchase.

The other contained a small Plexiglas box with air holes in the top. Within that box was a smaller receptacle, also of Plexiglas, with a fine mesh screen as the top cover. Inside, diligently pushing her little ebony fringed legs through the screen, was his very own black widow spider. Her beady eyes locked his, and he gave a shiver.

He closed the spider bag and placed them both on the passenger seat. As he eased into traffic, he kept looking nervously at the larger bag. Just then the phone rang.

"Hi sweetie," chirped Sheila. "Whatcha doing?"

"Finishing what I started," he replied grimly.

"Dontcha mean what WE started?" she questioned. "After all, we are in this together."

He looked at the spider bag with a strange expression, then shrugged. "I really don't see that I need you anymore," Neil responded.

Sheila almost shrieked. "Don't need me? Me? The expert? Listen, I've been successful at least three times, and you have botched it, buddy."

"Expert? The last milkshake didn't work Sheila, so now I have to do it another way."

"Well," she sulked, "You just walked in there bigger than life and tried to make him drink anti-freeze. You almost blew it totally. TOTALLY!"

"Okay, okay," Neil said soothingly, "I'll see you tonight and we can have dinner and talk about it. Right now I have to get somewhere."

Mollified, Sheila went into her little girl voice. "Okay snookums. See you later, alligator, you big handsome man."

Neil felt like throwing up, but he just gave it back with "After while, crocodile." She giggled and he hung up.

Now it was time to see Uncle Samuel at Meadowdale.

At Meadowdale there was a party going on. Instead of a Friday night movie, the staff had planned a Christmas dance. The local D.J. was playing oldies, like "Monster Mash", "Wipe Out" and "Blue Suede Shoes." The Independent Living folks were gyrating in styles from the Watusi and Stroll to the Monkey. The energy was electric.

There were also a group of folks from the Assisted Living building. The men were oogling the ladies who were swaying to the music. One old geezer was making circles in his walker around a rotund lady in a velvet sweat suit. She was dancing in tiny steps to keep up with his "dance."

The kitchen staff kept piling on the gluten-free cookies, veggie trays with radish roses, palm trees from bell peppers and carrots, and pineapple fish for the diabetics. The punch was flowing. Popcorn, chips, dips, and more were being devoured by the celebrants.

With only three days to Christmas, everyone was getting into the spirit of love, joy, and FOOD.

Darlene, in white boots, a tight red sweater and short black skirt, had no lack of partners. The old men kept cutting in on each other, and Darlene would wink and wiggle some more.

Charles and Laurel were sitting on the side of the room, sipping on punch and watching the fun.

"I sure do miss Laurel and Harting, the Snoop Sisters. That was something. I would love to have someone to sit and talk with, to share the rest of my life with. I am not that old yet, and life just isn't the same," Charles confided. "When I was despondent and depressed, just laying around was sufficient, but now, well, I am alive!"

Laurel didn't know how to respond, so she just smiled, nodded and touched his hand.

"When you meet someone who is warm, compassionate, intelligent, a bit feisty and full of vigor, it makes you realize how much you are missing. How much you wish that warmth were focused on one's self." Charles sighed. He looked dapper in his new suit and Christmas tie.

"I know the feeling, of missing a mate, of missing the companionship," Laurel agreed.

She took a long look at Charles. He wasn't a bad looking man, had financial security, and was willing to assist with the snooping. Was he hinting at something? Was he considering asking her to join him at Meadowdale.

"Let's dance," she said. Charles stood up and took her in his arms. Elvis was crooning "Love Me Tender." Laurel relaxed and moved to the soft rhythm of the music. Charles was a good dancer, if a bit reserved. Darlene whirled by in the arms of George, a big smile on her face. She gave Laurel a wink.

Upstairs, Olive was dealing with Walter, who had not been doing well for several days. He had caught a cold that went to his chest. Dr. Singh had even mentioned Hospice, but insisted he would keep Walter where he was. No one wanted to be moved to the Last Roundup.

Between coughing and dozing came fits of agitation and restlessness. Presently, he was demanding his "drinkie" for the second time in an hour. Olive heaved a heavy sigh, and headed for the alcove to get him another Ensure.

"Good night Olive," said Rose as she headed for the elevator. "Harold is finally asleep. Richard went back to his room about an hour ago. Because of the party there is just a skeleton crew tonight. I was just nervous about all the guests getting their dinner and meds. If it weren't for you and me helping out, our guys would have very little attention."

Olive nodded in agreement and walked with Rose toward the nurse's station. Sure enough, it was empty. Olive got a Styrofoam cup and poured herself some coffee.

"By the way," Rose said conspiratorially, "That aide from third floor was down here earlier while you were asleep. Apparently the boss, I guess Khan, wants to fast track two of the men on this floor up to the Last Roundup. There are two high profile guests in Assisted Living who they want to move here. I heard Nurse Bernice call Dr. Patel to confirm it. DeShawn looked in on Walter, but because you were in there, he passed."

"So who do you think is moving on?" asked Olive, as she sipped the dark brew.

"It looks like Major Dee Astor is a candidate for sure. His dementia is really overblown. I suspect Patel has been giving him something to make him more obvious. The other one was Mr. Obanion, the man in 213," suggested Rose, pulling her coat on.

Olive shook her head in disgust. "They don't worry about the medical condition, just the money they get from the room. Well, have a good night Rose, and drive safe."

"I will," Rose assured her as she signed the book. She pushed the button for the elevator and waved good bye to Olive, who was finishing her coffee as she headed for the alcove.

Driving into the Meadowdale parking garage, Neil noticed all the holiday decorations. He congratulated himself on his good luck. With the holiday distractions the staff was probably busy, and he could get to Uncle Samuel without being noticed.

Neil could hear the loud rocking music as he entered the foyer. Through the glass doors to the dining hall, he could see the old fogies dancing away like it was 1954. He laughed softly. "Perfect," he murmured and pushed the button for the elevator.

The door opened and Rose stepped out, her attention on her handbag as she searched for her keys. Neil slid past and quickly pushed the button to close the door, watching her back as Rose hurried out. It was dark and she wanted to get back to the duplex and get some rest.

"This can't be a bleak Christmas," Rose murmured. She was determined to make it special for her new friends and Harold. Rose pulled her grey herringbone coat a little tighter around her as she headed for her car.

Meanwhile, when the elevator door opened on Windom, Neil surveyed the room with a cursory glance. Sure enough, no one at the nurse's station. As he hurried down the hall to Uncle Samuel's room, he did not see Olive in the shadows of the alcove, but she saw him.

CHAPTER 28

Once Neil vanished into Room 211, Olive headed for the Nurse's Station.

The guest book was prominently place for all visitors to sign in when they arrived, who they were visiting, and the time they left. Rose was the last one to fill in her time, 7:20 P.M. Neil had not signed in. Obviously he was not planning to. Olive's eyes narrowed.

"I bet he has a nefarious purpose," she murmured to herself. Then she moved swiftly to give Walter his "drinkie" and settled into her recliner with her ears tuned to listen for trouble.

Trouble was just what Neil was up to.

When he entered Room 211, he tiptoed past Harold, who was sleeping with his back to Uncle Samuel's "private" room. Neil pulled the curtain closed and examined Uncle Samuel, who was also dozing, his mouth open, making huffing sounds.

Slowly Neil pulled the Plexiglas case from his coat pocket. The black widow looked angry, pushing at the screen, moving back and forth in the enclosed space. Her dark eyes glistened as she glared at him.

"Good, be mad, be very mad. Bite the first thing you

find, my beauty," Neil crooned as he gingerly removed the smaller box and placed the larger one on the side table. Carefully he unclasped the screen top and shook the shiny black insect onto his uncle's pillow.

The spider hesitated a moment, seeming to look around, then slowly crept toward Uncle Samuel's wisps of snowy hair. Neil was urging her on, as he often did his favorite horse at the track, with, "go, go, go!" He leaned forward, his eyes trained on her every movement.

Tentatively, she touched one strand and began to move closer to Samuel's balding scalp. "That's it!" Neil said louder leaning lower to the bed. "Bite him you…." Suddenly the spider halted. She spun around to look directly at Neil.

Stunned, he straightened up as the black widow sprang from the bed at him.

She hit the floor and began running toward his shoe. He shrieked and stomped solidly down on her tiny body, his heart in his throat.

Uncle Samuel sat up, rubbing his eyes. "Eh? What? Huh?" He seemed very confused.

Harold hollered from the other side of the curtain. "Heh! Keep it down!"

Neil dashed from the room, shoving the screened box in his pocket. He almost ran over Olive as she headed for Room 211.

"What's going on?" she demanded. Neil ran past her to the elevator without stopping to sign out of the book or answer her. He hurriedly jammed the numbers into the key pad.

Mykala came out of Major Astor's room and rushed to assist.

CHAPTER 29

Saturday morning Laurel woke up to see her phone blinking. She checked her text, and sure enough, Darlene had sent her a message. "Meeting at 10:00 upstairs. Urgent."

She text back, "See you then", and slowly got out of bed. This was not the way she planned to spend her Saturday two days before Christmas.

On her calendar, she had noted an auction at Stellar Auctions, which the man at Load and Lock had suggested. It was at two o'clock, which would give her plenty of time for the meeting at Meadowdale.

Laurel dressed quickly in a chic grey suit with a white silk blouse. She added a long silver necklace and changed everything into her grey Gucci knock off shoulder bag. Now she would fit in at the auction.

Laurel gulped down a protein shake and headed for the door.

In Windom Hall, Darlene had gathered two folding chairs from Calista to give seating in Walter's room. Olive wasn't about to leave his side. Her son Gordon and granddaughter Jean were scheduled to arrive after lunch. Walter no longer woke, no longer recognized her. He was fading fast. What a Christmas memory, Olive thought ruefully.

Rose had Richard and Harold at a table in the lounge. Harold was wearing his brown derby. The men were playing dominoes their way, making roads and walls as they ran the little cars from the game of LIFE around the table. Rose was smiling indulgently at her "guys".

Mike Minabird was wandering nearby, eyeing the salt and pepper shakers, when Marcia, an aide from Haliburton, arrived and steered him back toward his room.

Charles came up the elevator to see about Olive and Walter. He sat down near Olive and patted her hand. "Sorry old gal. This is tough. We are here for you, I guess you know that."

Olive smiled sadly back at him. "I know Charles. It is just so unfair. He was the nice one. I'm the pill."

"Some men like pills," Charles responded, smiling fondly at her.

Laurel arrived and joined the group. Olive sat in one recliner, Darlene in the other, with Charles and Laurel in the folding chairs. Calista looked into the room.

"Ya'll having a wake?" she inquired.

"I guess you would say that," Olive responded grumpily, and turned her attention to the group as she closed the door.

Calista smiled and strolled down the hall, adjusting the tiny receiver in her left ear.

"Okay," Charles said, getting their attention. "You know how I have found a hiding place behind the cockatiel cage near Khan's office? Well, I recorded a very interesting conversation Thursday just before Khan left for WinStar Casino for the weekend."

"You recorded a conversation? How?" brightened Olive, leaning forward with interest.

Darlene grinned. "When Richard was with me, I had one of those baby monitors in his room so I could cook and do whatever. Anyway, I still had it, so I gave it to Charles to use to bug Khan's office. I thought it would be a hoot."

"Wow," Laurel said, impressed. "That is very creative and highly illegal."

"I know," Charles replied proudly. "I've joined the Snoop Sisters in their nefarious shenanigans."

"And how did you record it?" asked Olive.

"Well, I sent away for one of those devices people use around the office. It was only forty dollars at Best Buy. Not the greatest, especially with the background noise of the birds and people walking by, but it sure caught interesting and incriminating information," boasted Charles, holding out the small black instrument.

He placed it on the end table and pushed PLAY. Turning the volume up to FULL, the group tilted their heads forward to listen.

The sound was scratchy but they listen with rapt attention. They were able to decipher most of what was being said. It was a conversation between Khan and Dr. Patel, and it appeared to be quite heated.

Patel: "Not again. Listen Khan, I cannot do any more over billing. As you know, there is an audit going on. I may be in trouble. WE may be in trouble."

Khan: "I need more money. Carmen is demanding a settlement for..(bird whistles). Just one more big win and I'll pay back what I've borrowed from you, and from here. I need five thousand by tonight when I leave."

Patel: "I don't have it. Deepika and the children have wiped me out for this trip home to India. I just don't have it. Why five thousand?"

Khan: "I have a marker for three thousand, and I can't get into a game for less than two thousand. Get it somehow."

Patel: "I can't get more than two thousand advance on my credit cards."

Khan: "Would you like the world to know how you have been over medicating those poor souls in LaRhonda? Or how you have moved people to the Memory Unit when they really are not severely demented? How you have certified deaths that are questionable?"

Patel: "On your instructions, Khan. I have proof that you requested a move for Mr. Kaiser to the Memory Unit tomorrow, and then a quick transfer to LaRhonda. Who is going to be HIS nephew when he passes so you can get the oil royalties? Eh? What if that bit of news were to get out?"

Khan: "Judge Cheatem has been working on that, and you will get your cut as usual. Right now I just need some hard cash."

Patel (big sigh): "I will go to ….(scratchy sounds) perhaps two thousand by tonight?"

Khan: "That will have to do. I can make a withdrawal from Rest Assured again. Damn, I owe them about ten thousand already, but this trip, (scratchy sounds, bird whistles, background noise)…what do you think?"

Patel: "I think this is the last time I am doing any of this. I am a doctor, sworn to do good. I don't know how I got sucked into (bird chattering, background noise)….and we are done."

(SOUND OF A DOOR CLOSING)

Charles turned off the recorder.

"That's all I got, but I think it is enough."

Olive sat back and grinned. "I think it is plenty. Obviously Khan has something on Dr. Patel that is pretty bad for Patel to do all those things against his better judgment."

"I know," Laurel said. "It sounds like Dr. Patel was probably a pretty good guy, but got in over his head. However, I can't feel sorry for him. Lives have been destroyed because of his medical malpractice."

Charles thought a minute. "With the patients here, it may be more like compassionate medical practice. No one is going to get well." He glanced over at Walter, Olives eyes following his.

"But Khan, good God!" exclaimed Darlene. "He robs the living and the dead."

"More than that," said Charles grimly. "Laurel, here is a list of items which have been reported as stolen from guests. Take it with you to the auction and see if any of them turned up there."

Laurel took the list and scanned it. Most of the items were from the Independent living section, but the Tiffany reading lamp from Samuel Prescott was also on the list.

Olive handed Laurel a plastic baggy, "See if you can get one of your police friends to dust this for finger prints. Neil left it in Samuel's room last night. I am not sure what it held, but I bet it wasn't good."

Laurel took the baggy with the Plexiglas box and slid it into her purse.

"Okay gang. I've got to go now, but please try to stay out of trouble." Laurel rose and headed for the door.

"What? And miss all the fun?" Darlene said impishly, pulling her smokes out of her pocket. She got up and started to fold up the chairs. As she carried them to the closet in the hall, she saw Calista walking behind Laurel.

Laurel signed the book and was waiting for the elevator when Calista walked up and held out her hand.

"I need that baggy, Miss Laurel."

Laurel looked startled. "The baggy?"

Calista moved in front of the elevator.

"That's right, missy. The baggy Olive gave you. That is evidence. I can run it better than you can. Besides, if you don't, I can ask you not to return, since you don't have a resident here."

"How did you know about the baggy?" Laurel inquired in amazement.

"You Snoops Sister ain't the only ones with a bug," Calista grinned, gesturing to her ear.

"OH! So the buggers have been bugged."

"That's right," smugly Calista replied as Laurel handed her the baggy. "And I'll have Charles' little tape device next."

"You are making a big mistake," Laurel said. "There are bad things happening here and we plan on stopping them."

"I know," said Calista sadly, "I know."

CHAPTER 30

As Laurel was exiting the elevator, she met Gordon Harting, Olive's son. He looked distressed.

"Gordon, I just left your mom and dad. I am so glad you got here." Laurel said gently.

"Thank you Laurel. I know mom has been counting on your friendship here. How is dad doing?"

"Not too good, Gordon," she replied with a sad smile. "I've got to run, but call me if you need anything. We all love your parents."

Gordon entered the elevator and the door slid shut.

Laurel hurried to the Stellar Auction House where the preview was being held prior to the auction itself. She checked her list with the offerings, and sure enough, the Tiffany lamp was there, along with a signed Dali print, and a Waterford glass candy dish from a Miss Templeton. The oriental vase was a maybe, as there was no photograph as proof.

Laurel went to the payment window.

"I would like to inquire about the Tiffany lamp. Can you tell me who brought it in? I collect Tiffany and would like to see if they have any more available."

The woman opened her book. "I don't normally do this,

but since it is Christmas, and the man said he really needed the money, maybe it will help you both. Let's see, it was a Mr. DeShawn Brown, in Garland. I can give you a phone number," the woman said, helpfully.

"I would appreciate that," Laurel said, as she pulled pen and paper out of her handbag. "That was DeShawn Brown?" The woman nodded, and recited the phone number.

Laurel thanked her and wandered toward the auction room.

"Auction is starting in thirty minutes" the announcer intoned. Laurel got a number and took her seat. Obviously she would not be bidding, but she wanted to record all the sales on the stolen items.

An hour later she turned in her paddle and left for home, with four of the nine items listed having sold for a total of $1,642.00. Not bad for a day's work. Laurel wondered how much of it would be split with Khan.

She called Darlene. "Can you see if there is a DeShawn Brown on staff at Meadowdale? I haven't heard of him before, but I imagine this is an inside job."

Within thirty minutes Darlene called her back. "He works nights on LaRonda. I think he is just an aide. It sounds like he has a second job moonlighting as a cat burglar." Darlene giggled at her own joke.

"Well, the jig is about to be up. I took photos of the items, and the paddle numbers of each of the purchasers. I bet the police would like to look into this. At least Load and Lock is not crooked," Laurel said bitterly.

"Load and Lock, what a name. Can you imagine their ad? "We aim to please," or "No one will rifle through your stuff." Darlene was laughing again. "And they could have a target with bullet holes as a sign."

"Oh Darlene, you have more fun with nothing than most folks do with something," Laurel laughed. "How is Richard?"

"Better than Walter. They've called in Hospice for him, and both kids came in today. Olive is stoic. She expects the worst," Darlene confided. "At least Dr. Singh is on it, not Patel. He and Khan are gone this weekend."

"Good for them," said Laurel. "Hopefully those two will be gone for a long time when we get through with them."

"So, what is the plan," asked Darlene. "Who are we going to tell?"

"I think we are going to have to contact the brothers," Laurel said firmly. After she hung up, Laurel pulled a T.V. dinner from the freezer and settled down for a quiet Saturday night.

Olive was finally resting while their son Gordon and his daughter, Jean sat vigil with Walter. Jean had left baby Troy with his dad. Two days before Christmas, and Walter was on hospice. This was a going to be a blue, blue Christmas.

Darlene had snuggled on the bed with Richard for a few minutes, until he fell asleep. She knew the men downstairs considered her a flirt, but her heart belonged only to her Richard.

Life was not fair, but it was what it was, and Darlene had always made the best of it. She wiped away a few tears as she headed for the portico for her last cigarette of the night.

In room 211 Rose had hugged Harold one more time, and made the lonely drive back to the duplex. If only she could stay with Harold like Olive did with Walter, she thought. But, financially it was impossible.

They were lucky Harold was in a shared room, although Samuel Prescott thought he was in a private room. Rose smiled to herself and counted her blessings.

The night was going to be long and quiet on Windom Hall.

But it was going to be a rocky one in the high rent district on Lemon Avenue in Dallas.

Sheila Bunachellie was sprawled in a red leather recliner in Neil's apartment as he paced angrily back and forth.

"I can't believe I wasted sixty bucks on that stupid spider. It seemed so simple." Neil fumed again. "It was right there, at his head, getting ready to bite him, when it turned on ME!"

"Calm down sweetie," she crooned. "I'm here with a great Plan B."

Neil stopped and glared at her. "What, another Plan B?"

She smiled confidently. "I have this baggy of Mary Jane. We are baking brownies for Uncle Samuel."

"Alice B Toklas? Marijuana? That's your answer," Neil blurted, dumbfounded.

Sheila sighed. "Listen, I've been reading up on the old geezers with Alzheimer's. When they eat too many brownies, they start to act erratic, not mellow. Then, the doctor, not knowing what is going on, gives them heavy sedatives, which pushes their heart to the edge. Now, if that doesn't finish him off, we give him a tiny injection of this special potion here and the doctor takes all the blame."

She held up a vial of a liquid, and a syringe.

"The doctor, of course, doesn't want to go under the

bus, so he lists it as a heart attack. It worked once for me, but unfortunately the relatives interfered, so I didn't get anything but the diamonds he had given me," Sheila said as she held up her left hand sporting two large, flashy diamond rings.

"Okay, let's do it," Neil agreed.

Languidly, Sheila rose and headed for the kitchen, where she unpacked a paper grocery sack with a brownie mix, eggs, oil and a square 8 x 8 baking pan. Soon the kitchen smelled of delicious chocolate, with a slight herbal overtone.

"Christmas is coming," Sheila sang as she pulled the brownies out of the oven and set them to cool. "And, going in late will work the best."

Neil suddenly became nervous. "They lock the doors at ten o'clock. It is already almost nine, and I want to give them to him right before the change of shift."

"Well sugar, go in now, stay in the bathroom downstairs until after ten, then go upstairs while the nurses are giving their report and make sure he eats several. Watch out, and get back out before they see you."

Neil got into his silver Lexus and roared into the night. Meadowdale was aglow with Christmas lights on Julep, the Assisted Living building. Giant wreaths graced the doors of the main building.

It was nine fifty-two when Neil entered the building with twelve warm, chocolate brownies zipped in a quart bag under his jacket. He slipped into the public restroom downstairs and locked himself in one of the stalls.

He stared at his watch, willing the minutes to pass. He heard the elevator doors open and close four times. Finally it was ten-forty. Time to go upstairs, he told himself.

Looking around the vestibule, Neil observed it was empty. The dining hall was dark, and the dimly lit hallway to the Independent Living rooms was ghostly quiet as he pushed the button on the elevator. This was it. Another Plan B was underway.

CHAPTER 31

Neil knew the shift had changed because he heard the chatter of the aides heading for their lockers and the time clock ding before he opened the bathroom door. As the elevator rose, he held his breath. What about the nurse at the desk? He had not planned that far.

Fortunately for him, Nurse Bernice and Nurse Betty were gathered for evening report with Willie and the other two night aides. Their heads bent over the charts, no one noticed Neil slip into the room closest to the elevator. He watched through a crack in the door until Nurse Bernice left, and Nurse Betty headed for down the South hall with Willie to check on Major Astor.

The coast being clear, Neil hurried to Room 211, walked quietly past Harold, and pushed back the curtain to see his Uncle Samuel snoring away.

He shook his uncle awake.

"Whhhh, ah, bzqk?" Samuel muttered. "Wha, wha?"

"Look Uncle. Brownies! Yummy brownies! Here, eat one, eat several," Neil urged, pushing a thick chocolate slice in front of his confused uncle's face.

Latesha Vernon, one of the night aides, had heard a voice. She pulled back the curtain to see what was happening.

"It is past visiting hours, sir," she said sternly. Then she got a whiff of the chocolate brownies, and a scent of something else, something she recognized instantly.

"What do you have there," she said, with a lilt in her voice. "Are those brownies?"

Neil looked nervous, embarrassed and stuttered, "Yes, ye-ye-yes. A gift for Uncle Samuel. His favorite."

Latesha held out her hand. "It is a bit late for a snack, but if you leave them with me, I'll make sure they get eaten."

"You'll see *he* gets them? All of them?" Neil asked eagerly. "I want him to know I brought him his favorites, for Christmas, you know."

"I'll make sure he knows," was the silky reply. Latesha smiled at him, her eyelashes blinking as she took the bag.

Neil heaved a sigh of relief. It was on their hands now, if Uncle passed quietly from brownie overload. He smiled gratefully at Latesha as he left for the elevator. Again, luck was with him. No one was at the nurse's station, and the foyer downstairs was empty.

Neil was seated in his Lexus before he realized his hands were shaking. Tomorrow the doctor would call to say Uncle had taken a turn for the worst, and he would react with sadness. Neil suspected he could be a very convincing actor.

When he got back to the apartment, Sheila was waiting, expectantly.

"Did you do it? Did he eat them?"

Neil hesitated. "Well, he ate one, and then the aide came in. She agreed to give him the rest tomorrow, as a treat from me."

Sheila's brow furrowed. "Did she now. And you believed her?"

"Why would she lie," he said, exasperated. "What else could I do?"

"Well," purred Sheila, "Tomorrow we will pay a little visit to Uncle and make sure he goes over the edge, won't we?"

"Whatever," agreed Neil. "Now, I'm going to bed. You do whatever you want."

With that, he went to his room, shut the door, and flopped fully clothed on the bed, hoping to hear the sound of the door as she left. He was not disappointed.

Latesha had eaten half a brownie when Nurse Betty found her.

"What are you doing?" Betty demanded.

"Just having a snack," replied Latesha, smirking a bit.

"Well, you can wait until break time. You just got here, and there are rounds, young lady. Rounds which need to be done BEFORE break!" Nurse Betty took the bag with the brownies and set them on top of the file cabinet at the nurse's station, then herded Latesha down the hall to the linen closet where freshly laundered sheets were waiting to be put away.

Latesha cast a glance back down the hall toward the brownies, sighed, and went to work.

She was too busy to hear the ding of the elevator as DeShawn came down to see if there were any notes on patients to go up to LaRonda. As he stepped into the nurse's station, he spied the brownies. His trained olfactory nerves were smitten with the herbal overtones, and DeShawn grinned as he swiftly snatched the bag and slipped it into the large pocket of his dark blue scrubs.

The light from under the door of Walter's room shown dimly.

Olive and her granddaughter, Jean, had finally gone to sleep in the bed behind the curtain while Gordon dozed in the recliner. Mr. Harvey, the Hospice worker, sat vigil stoically in the recliner closest to Walter.

Time was short. Walter had caught a cold, which quickly turned to bronchitis and was threatening pneumonia. Olive had instructed Mr. Harvey to wake her if Walter seemed close to the end. It was terribly silent night in Windom Hall for the Hartings.

As DeShawn exited the elevator on LaRonda he was almost dancing.

"Lookee, lookee. Party time!" he sang out exultantly, holding up the bag of chocolate treats. Nurse Tina Racket and Carla DeSoto looked up from the charts.

"Brownies?" Tina inquired. "What's up?"

Carla opened the bag, smelled the chocolate and marijuana, and grinned.

"Get out the rum and Coca-cola. I've got chips and cookies in the file cabinet. DeShawn, do you still have some pork rinds? We are going to need munchies tonight."

Nurse Tina smiled. "Do the rounds quickly, then we can relax and enjoy a snack."

Carla took the east hall, while DeShawn did a quick check on the patients in the west hall. They met back at the nurse's station in record time. Most of the patients were so sedated that the night shift was a breeze.

"Okay, now, we share and share alike," instructed Nurse Racket, dividing the thick brown, fragrant squares. She passed out Dixie cups filled with Bacardi and Coke. Cookies, chips and an open bag of pork rinds were piled on her desk. It was Christmas, after all, time to celebrate.

An hour later they were raiding the bedside drawers of all the patients to find anything from lemon drops to Altoids. Carla even snatched a bottle of fruit-flavored Tums.

DeShawn threw back the last of the Bacardi and sought the only empty bed on the Unit. The last he had seen of Carla, she had been going through drawers again, in case they had missed anything edible.

At six forty-five A.M. the sound of the elevator woke Nurse Racket. She raised her head from her desk, pushed the hair out of her face and looked up. Her mascara made raccoon circles around her eyes, and there were chocolate crumbs on her desk.

The trash around the waste basket screamed "party time." A green Bacardi bottle sat like a tiny Christmas tree among the discarded food wrappers.

The morning crew stood staring at her.

"Morning, ya'll," she greeted them with a sloppy smile. Then, catching herself, she cleared her throat, sat up straight, and reached for her charts. "Uh, I guess it is time to do report."

"And where are DeShawn and Carla?" inquired Wylie, the Med Clerk.

"I'm not sure," admitted Nurse Racket. She appeared confused. "I left them here somewhere."

One of the aides went in search of Carla and DeShawn.

Morning had come, and several of the patients were stirring. It was time to change Depends and prepare for the breakfast trays to arrive.

Charlotte found Carla sitting cross-legged on the floor at the end of the west hall, staring vacantly at her phone as it played a Youtube video of kittens dancing. At Charlotte's urging, Carla got up unsteadily, her left leg still asleep.

They found DeShawn sprawled asleep on the only empty bed on the Unit, a crumpled bag of pork rinds beside him. Wylie shook him awake.

Embarrassed, DeShawn sat up. "Uh, I'm not feeling too good. I think I'm coming down with somethin'," he muttered.

"I think it was something you ate," Wylie said, smugly, holding up the rind bag.

DeShawn huffed, and stood up, brushing off his scrubs. "Time to go. Hope you have a good shift, my friend. I'm going home and crash."

"Call before you come in on Wednesday," called Nurse Racket sternly to him. "You may not have a job." He gave her a hard look.

"What about you?" he shot back.

"I was at my desk. I must have dozed off about five A.M. after my last rounds. That's when I lost track of you and Carla. Looks like you two had quite a party." Nurse Racket pointed to the waste basket, and exchanged a knowing look with Nurse Headly, who had just stepped off the elevator.

"What happened?" Nurse Headly asked Wylie.

"Looks like Carla and DeShawn waited until Racket took a snooze, then they did a little nippin' and sippin'," Wylie offered, looking to Nurse Racket for approval. She smiled at him broadly and agreed.

"Are you going to write them up?" Headly asked Nurse Racket.

"Of course," she said primly, wiping her mouth on a

tissue as she got her purse. "I'll turn it in on Monday. No, that's Christmas. I'll turn it in Tuesday morning."

She looked around. "You are all witnesses, right?"

"Right," they agreed in unison, as Carla and DeShawn slunk toward the elevator under Nurse Headly's blazing glare.

The worst was yet to come for DeShawn.

CHAPTER 32

Latesha was waiting for DeShawn when he entered the employee lounge. She stood by his locker, tapping her foot.

"And where are my brownies?" she demanded hotly.

"What makes you think I took them?" he responded.

"Well," she said," everyone knows you are a thief. I saw you sneak that lamp out last week. And the grapevine is hot with the Amy scandal. I know you set that one up too."

DeShawn looked at her in disbelief. "You know about that?"

"We all know about that. You are going down, boy. Big time." Latesha laughed.

"And, by the way, I stole those brownies from old man Prescott in the first place!" She giggled again.

"If I'm losing my job, I'm taking you with me," he fumed.

"Ain't goin' happen DeShawn. You bite this one by yourself. And also, by the way, Walter Harting won't be doing a transfer to LaRonda. He died last night."

At that, Latesha flounced past him into the morning light, leaving DeShawn shaking his head.

The atmosphere was solemn on the Windom Hall.

The staff had become quite fond of Olive and Walter.

Theirs was a unique situation at Meadowdale, a husband and wife sharing a room on the Memory Care Unit. It had always been strictly for men, but Olive had given them so much relief in her care not only for Walter but for so many of the other guests, it was first tolerated, then welcomed.

Now an era seemed to be over.

After Dr. Singh had come to pronounce the death, the Coroner's office was contacted and Walter's body was removed to the Infirmary.

Gordon told his mother he would take them to his room at the Hyatt Regency, where they could finally shower and rest before making further arrangements.

Christmas was tomorrow. There would be no funeral before Wednesday, and Olive was unsure of her next move. Of course she couldn't stay in their old room on Windom Hall. But, she didn't want to leave Meadowdale and her support group.

"Just sleep on it, Mom," encouraged Gordon. "Things will look different tomorrow."

As the little group headed for the elevator, Rose, Harold, Darlene and Richard were waiting. The ladies surrounded Olive to hug her and whisper words of comfort while Harold held out his hand to Gordon. Jean stood uncertain for a minute, until Darlene turned and engulfed her in an affectionate bear hug.

"We're here, old Dear," she said to Olive. "Go get some rest. The Snoop Sisters will be back in business before you know it."

Olive smiled weakly at them, then asked, "Where is Charles? Does he know?"

Darlene shook her head. "He was still asleep this morning. I'll tell him when he gets up, kiddo."

Gordon took Olive's overnight bag and led her to the elevator.

Downstairs Charles was busy wrapping the last of his gifts for his Meadowdale friends. Dora, one of the aides, had started a personal shoppers business for the guests on Independent Living who wanted help choosing the appropriate items.

He carried his large holiday bag to the elevator and whistled as he journeyed upward to Windom Hall.

The elevator doors opened to a sad scene. Darlene was comforting a sobbing Rose while Richard and Harold stood, confused and worried.

Charles signed in and listed Olive as the guest he was visiting. Nurse Yvonne shook her head and waved toward the cluster of his friends.

"Walter died last night. Olive has left with her family. I'm so sorry," she looked down at her desk, then back up, tears glistening. "They will be missed around here."

"Oh no!" Charles exclaimed. Darlene looked up and saw him, and noticed the brightly colored bag bulging with gifts.

"Hey kiddo, she asked about you before they left. What's up?"

"I was bringing Christmas!" Charles said, then apologized, "I guess I am too late."

Darlene sighed, "Well, maybe we need a little Christmas cheer. Let's go to the dining room and see what you got."

Darlene took Richard by the arm and led him to the tables. Rose and Harold joined them as Charles opened his pack.

"For you, Rose, a carpet bag to carry your knitting. You can stop using a plastic Kohl's sack." She hugged the beautifully embroidered bag and smiled at Charles. "Thank you, it's perfect."

Charles pulled out another brightly wrapped package, and handed it to Harold. "Here are the New York Times, the Washington Journal, the Los Angeles Times and the San Francisco Free Press. I think you'll have fun reading these each morning."

Harold ripped open the wrappings and lifted up a stack of news papers. Adjusting his hat, Harold sat down to look through them. He could no longer read because of his eyes, but he loved leafing through the pages, pretending to absorb all the news that was fit to print.

"Me next, me next," insisted Richard, holding out his arms expectantly.

The colorful bag Charles handed to Richard had a set of headphones filled with music. Darlene helped him adjust them. Soon Richard's head was bobbing in time with the beat, a big grin on his face.

"You bug!" Darlene exclaimed, hugging Charles. "You knew just what he loved most, music."

Charles smiled at her. "And what do you love, dear heart? How about these?"

Her package held a shoe box, with lovely red Jimmy Choo Anouk Suede Pumps in her size.

"Oh my, Charles!" she squealed. "I LOVE them!" She hugged Charles and kissed him on the cheek. Looking past them, Richard smiled gently as he rocked back and forth to the music only he could hear.

He had two more gifts in his bag.

"This was for Olive. Will she be back?" he asked with concern, lifting out a small, flat box.

"She has to settle something about where to live now that Walter is gone. Of course the room has to be emptied in three days, and I'm not sure what she will do" admitted Darlene, her eyes misted over. "I am going to miss our group."

"It's not over until it is over," Charles said grimly.

And it wasn't over yet, although no one knew that for sure.

CHAPTER 33

Christmas Eve day broke with Laurel was eating a toasted bagel with cream cheese and watching the news. She felt she really should call Olive or Darlene and see how Walter was, but she dreaded hearing bad news. It was too soon after Martin was gone to face more sadness.

The phone rang. After two rings, Laurel pressed the green button.

"Hello," she said quietly.

"Hey doll face, this is Darlene. They are having a fab brunch down here on Indie, and I really wish you could join me. It's Sunday, after all."

"I know, and I'm going to candlelight service at 5 P.M. at Our Lady, you know the one," sighed Laurel, with no enthusiasm.

"Well get your butt down here, NOW!" demanded Darlene. "Walter died last night so Olive went with Gordon and Jean to the Hyatt to rest. Richard is sitting with Rose and Harold. As you know, they can't come. Charles handed out Christmas presents, although none of us thought of that. He has one for you. And I am bored. B-O-R-E-D. BORED!"

That brought a smile to Laurel's face. Good old Darlene

knew how to make a party happen even if there wasn't a reason. Laurel sighed heavily, then straightened up.

"Okay, give me thirty minutes. What time is it now?"

Darlene reported, "It is two freckles past a hair, or ten thirty, in earth talk. Anyway, the shindig starts in an hour, so you are fine. I just need a human to talk to or I will go out of my skull!"

Laurel laughed. "I think there are at least sixty humans on your Independent wing, maybe more. And what about Charles? He surely is human."

In hushed tone Darlene shared, "You won't believe what he gave me for Christmas. Fab red Jimmy Choo Anouk suede pumps. I've been coveting them for weeks, but at $550, all I could do was drool over their photo in the Neiman Marcus wish book. Now I am nervous he may be looking for something in return."

"Well, he did share with me he was lonely now that he has decided to live." Laurel added, "I think he was coming on to me at the dance, you know, hinting that we might be a good match."

"Really?" Darlene said in disbelief. "You and Charles? Are you kidding?"

"What's so weird about that" demanded Laurel hotly. "Don't you think I'm still young enough to want to date?"

"Well," drawled Darlene, "You may be young enough, honey, but ol' Charlie boy is a bit of a snob and an intellectual. He isn't turned by a pretty face."

Laurel pondered that input for a minute.

"I'm on my way in ten," she finally told Darlene. "Save me a place."

"Sure thing, girl friend," Darlene replied, and they both hung up.

When the phone rang at the nurse's station a bit later at Windom Hall, the only person to answer was an aide from Julep who was filling in at the last minute. Cathy grabbed the phone and said, "Hello, Windom Hall, may I help you?"

"Yes, this is Neil Armstrong, and I was inquiring about my Uncle, Samuel Prescott. Can he have visitors?"

"Of course," responded the harried aide. "Visiting hours are from ten A.M. to seven P.M. today. It is Christmas Eve, and we want to make sure the guests are all snuggled safe in their beds for Santa." She then shouted at someone down the hall, "Hold your horses, I'm coming."

Back to the phone. "Is that all?"

"Uh, has the doctor been to see him today," Neil inquired tentatively.

"Look, it is Christmas Eve. No doctors, and just a few of us doing all the work. Got to go." Cathy hung up and hurried down the hall to see why Mr. Weston was yelling.

Neil hung up and looked thoughtful.

No doctors, a skeleton staff, and a night when no one would notice anything. It was now or never. He picked up the cell phone again and dialed Sheila.

"Okay my dear. Another Plan B I think. Do you still have that vial of stuff?" Neil asked.

"Oh yes, I have a vial and I know how to use it." Sheila laughed a throaty laugh. "It has worked wonders in the past. This is where I shine. Now, do you have a small pistol, or do I need to bring mine?"

"What for?" Neil asked nervously. "I don't think we need a gun."

"Insurance, sweet cheeks." Sheila replied. "It just makes a small popping sound. Close range kind of gun, a little 32 caliber KEL-tec like I have for personal protection."

"Whatever," Neil said. "Visiting hours are over at 7 P.M. tonight. I thought we could go about six or six-thirty and finish this. Tomorrow is Christmas, and the regular staff is not there. It could go unnoticed for a couple of days if we are lucky. Then, I will be SO so broken hearted."

Sheila giggled gleefully. "I am so ready for this. I'll be over at five-thirty and we can ride together. This is a two person job. You administer the stick in his foot while I cover his mouth in case he hollers, then we walk out saying "Merry Christmas" to cover any noise he makes while he convulses."

"Convulses? Does it hurt?" Neil said, horrified.

"What's your problem. You want him dead. And dead is what he will be. Suck it up, buttercup. You want his money, I want your money, we both need him dead to get it." The lilt was gone from Sheila's voice and it was hard and cold. Neil shivered at the thought.

It was decision time.

When he hung up, Neil looked at his last credit card bill. So far, he was in debt to Visa for six thousand plus, and his Master Card was headed for the max his credit would allow. The decision had been made.

At the Hyatt, Gordon had made phone calls to all his relatives and his parent's friends in Elgin, Austin and Forney.

Both his parents had received their degrees from the University of Texas in Austin, and he had grown up in Elgin until his mother received her first position as a school principal in Forney. The move was easy. Walter had been a high school math teacher, and the transfer to a rural school had been a happy one. No big cities for them again.

Olive had decided that both she and Walter would be cremated, but the plot they had purchased years ago in Elgin would be the site of a dual tombstone. Intellectually Olive knew neither of them would be there, but it was a place for the ritual of rememberance. That was important to Gordon and his daughter Jean.

"Someday Troy may want to see where you were raised," Jean explained to Gordon. "This grave will be an anchor. When you are gone, we can add your name too."

Gordon nodded, finally understanding.

"Mom, do you want the service here where your friends are, or down in Elgin, where family is?" Gordon asked, getting out his yellow legal pad.

"Let's do the actual ceremony to honor Walter in Elgin, where we lived the longest. It is close enough friends from Forney can come, and I know my friends at Meadowdale will understand." Olive looked at Gordon for a long time.

"Where should I be? I mean, Elgin was so long ago, and Forney isn't where I want my last stop to be. Neither of you live near there. I've sort of made a new set of old friends right here. Would you mind if I moved into Independent Living at Meadowdale? I think it would be easiest for all concerned." She looked beseechingly at Gordon.

Jean nodded. "I can go for that. We can come visit a couple of times a year, and Skype. You know, the computer thing where we can see each other as we talk. That way you won't miss Troy's milestones."

Gordon was quick to agree. "You won't have to change your driver's license or really, your address. We would move over the things you want to keep, and fill in with a few new pieces for an office. I know you miss that the most. Two big book cases, and a better television."

They were all smiling by now.

It felt good to have the decision made. There was only one more decision hanging in the balance.

Laurel had gotten a phone call from her son Derreck as she was heading out the door.

"Mom, I've sold my condo and am in partnership with Kenji Takada, a Japanese businessman who is backing my restaurant. We just purchased a building on North Highland in Hollywood. It is called the Alhambra. There is an apartment in it for you and one for me. We are putting in an awesome Sushi bar on the ground floor. I am stoked. Totally stoked. With Dad gone, you need somewhere to be."

"That's something to think about, Derreck. I am not sure right now what to do," replied Laurel, wondering what brought this on.

"If you have any of that insurance money left, or whatever you got on the condo, I could use about ten thousand to seal the deal. Then you would never have to pay rent again. How about it?" Derreck was almost wheedling.

Laurel paused. She had less than twenty thousand left, but now she wasn't paying for Martin's care, it might not be a bad idea.

"Let me think about it and call you tomorrow," she said. "Love you, and Merry Christmas."

Sometimes a decision deferred is also a decision.

CHAPTER 34

The brunch had been very pleasant, and the company was uplifting. Darlene kept the conversation going with all those around, including George in his plaid bow tie and Myrtle, who had put a spring of holly in her grey bun.

After dessert several of them went to the tables in back and broke out a game of rummy. Around two o'clock Charles joined them. He had a bag with him that he slung under his chair.

It turned out that both Charles and Darlene had the killer instinct when it came to cards, and Laurel soon bowed out. "I've got to go to the candlelight service," she apologized. "I think I'll head over early."

"Before you go I have something for you," Charles said, pulling the bag from under his chair. "Merry Christmas."

Laurel took the bag and looked cautiously inside. It was the lovely leather Kate Spade satchel she had mentioned to Olive. A real beauty, and perfect for a legal secretary. At nearly $300 it had been light years from her budget.

When Laurel threw her arms around Charles and kissed him on the cheek, she felt him stiffen. "Thank you, thank you," she said with a smile as he blushed.

"I knew you wanted it, and after all, what are friends

for?" He moved back from her, a bit uncomfortable at the display of affection.

"And about your question, well, I think I may be moving to Los Angeles where my son has a new Sushi restaurant. I hope you can find the person you are looking for to share, well, talk with, Charles." Laurel said apologetically.

He was chagrinned. "I didn't know I had asked you a question, but I think you are making the right choice."

She smiled at him again.

"Bye everyone. Have fun, and Darlene, don't cheat. You know you should be dealing cards in Vegas the way you play."

Darlene and the gang waved goodbye and turned back to their rummy game.

Before she left Meadowdale, Laurel went up to Windom Hall to say goodbye to Rose.

"My dear, can you come back by and bring a Dr. Pepper in a bottle for Harold? He misses those, and, well, if you can find it, a fruit cake for me. I had a friend who always sent me one from Collin Street Bakery. It was our big celebration from Christmas to New Years, eating on one of those tasty fruit cakes. I don't know why people don't like them." Rose added with a bit of a frown.

"Will do," Laurel said, kissing her on the cheek. Rose was knitting a muffler in brilliant blues and forest green, pulling the yard to her needles from the handy knitting bag Charles had given her for Christmas. Harold was quietly sorting his newspapers.

From the other side of the curtain, the T.V. blared a science program about white salamanders found deep underground.

Laurel raised her eyebrows in question.

"Oh, that Mr. Prescott loves the science programs. That is all he watches. If they aren't on, the T.V. isn't on. When they are on, we ALL get to hear it," complained Rose. "I am leaving at seven tonight and not coming back until after lunch tomorrow. I need a break."

Laurel buttoned her jacket, ready for the chilly weather outside. "I'll see you before seven tonight with a Dr. Pepper and a fruitcake," she promised.

As she signed out of the visitor log, Laurel realized tonight might be her last trip to Windom Hall. With Olive moving somewhere else, there was really nothing to call her back. And now that she had decided to move to Los Angeles to be with Derreck, her focus had changed.

"You can't drive looking only in the rear view mirror," she told herself as she left Meadowdale to get her supplies and go to the candle light service at Our Lady of the Perpetual Virgin.

At five o'clock on the dot Sheila arrived at Neil's apartment, dressed in black slacks, black Sketchers and a black North Face hoody. Her hair was pulled up in a knot on top of her head and she had on black rimmed glasses.

"What are you, the Mafia?" Neil asked.

"No, just want to be able to make a quick getaway. I have the vial and syringe in the pouch of my hoody. Is that what you are wearing?" Sheila looked in surprise at his green Christmas sweater with an appliquéd reindeer.

"I thought it was festive," he responded, defensively.

Sheila sighed. "Whatever. Let's get this over with."

Neil went back to his room and changed into a black

button down shirt and black leather jacket. He had traded his Stefano Berner dress shoes for a pair of Niki tennis shoes.

"Better," Sheila agreed as she slung a small leather backpack over her shoulder. "We can stop at Chipotle on the way."

They pulled into the nearly deserted parking lot at six P.M. sharp and headed for the main lobby.

Christmas dinner had been served at five-thirty for all residents who were still there for the holidays. In the dining room about a dozen residents were still visiting with each other and lingering over coffee and dessert. No one noticed Sheila and Neil as they went to the elevator.

Once on Windom Hall, a passing aide they didn't recognize signaled to them from the nurse's station.

"You need to sign in please," she chortled. "All visitors out by seven so our guests can take their rests."

"Obviously a poet," suggested Sheila. The aide just smiled broadly as they filled out the book.

In Room 211, Rose was dozing in the recliner, her knitting forgotten on her lap. Harold was lying asleep on the bed, his grey Homburg Fedora with the little red feather perched on his forehead, moving up and down the rhythm of his breathing.

Sheila and Neil moved quietly past them to Uncle Samuel's bedroom. Neil pulled the curtain and Sheila moved to the end of the bed. Samuel was wide awake and staring at them suspiciously.

"Who are you and what do you want?" he demanded.

"It's me Uncle Samuel," Neil assured him. "We've come to wish you Merry Christmas."

"I don't need any of your damn cheer. Get out." Samuel

said harshly, as he pushed the button to raise the bed into a sitting position.

At the end of the bed, Sheila had tugged the blanket and sheet up and was trying to grab his foot.

"Tell her to get away from me," Samuel barked. "That painted hussy. Get her out of here." Samuel was kicking at her as she tried again and again to secure a grip on his heel.

Neil pressed his uncle's shoulders down against the bed.

"We will be out of here in a minute, Uncle. You should have eaten the brownies."

"What brownies? What in blazes?" his uncle was truly confused now and relaxed a minute.

Sheila had filled the syringe but Samuel was moving his feet to kick her again, and she was getting frustrated.

"Neil, you come do this and I'll hold him down with a pillow if I have to."

Neil moved quickly to the foot of the bed while Sheila handed him the syringe.

"Just put it in his ankle and plunge it," she instructed.

Both of them had lost awareness of the couple on the other side of the curtain, but Rose was wide awake now, and scared. Harold opened his eyes and looked at her. She shushed him with a finger to her lips and motioned for him to stay still.

Then she slipped out into the hall to find help.

Sheila grabbed a pillow, forcing it onto Samuel's face. He struggled and turned, trying to avoid suffocation and at the same time keep his feet moving, but it was a losing battle.

Neil caught is left foot and held it long enough to get the syringe down to his ankle when the curtain bowed in and the heavy armoire crashed directly down on him. The weight of the television was the last thing he felt.

Sheila sprang back in surprise as the "wall" of armoire and grey curtain collapsed on Neil and the bed revealing Calista and Nurse Bernice with Rose Goldberg gaping at her.

Reaching into her hoody, Sheila pulled out her little 32 caliber KEL-tec and aimed it at Rose. Harold stood panting behind her from the exertion of shoving over the bookcase and armoire.

"Get back!" Sheila demanded. "Get back or someone dies."

Calista's eyes narrowed. "I wouldn't do that if I were you," she said in a low voice. "Sheila Bunachellie, or should I say Sheila Krutznuckle, the police have been called. You are wanted in two states for the murder of your husbands. Don't add another to your rap sheet."

The gun waved back and forth on the little group. Behind her Samuel Prescott groaned in pain from a broken leg. The armoire had pinned him to the bed when it crushed his nephew.

"Then you realize I have no qualms about using this little six shot pistol on the lot of you," Sheila hissed. "I just want to walk out of here, no questions asked. We all live."

Rose looked at Calista. "How do you know about this lady?"

"She ain't no lady," responded Calista. "I'm on the Police Reserve, and I was hired by the Markowitz family to ferret out the illegal activity here at Meadowdale. It is a black eye on their Corporate image."

Nurse Bernice looked from the gun to Calista. "Uh, and you've found some?" Nurse Bernice looked nervous.

"Yeah Bernice. I've found quite a bit. I doubt if Mr. Rupert will be taking you out again, if you get my drift."

Sheila was furious. "Shut up and get out of my way so I can leave. NOW!"

Sirens screamed in the background.

Just as she raised her pistol and pointed it at Calista, Samuel swung his pillow with all his might and struck Sheila in the back of her head, throwing her off balance. As she stumbled forward, Calista had her in a headlock and Nurse Bernice wrenched the pistol from her hand.

Calista had Sheila down and was sitting on her when the police showed up in the doorway, pistols drawn. "Pete, just need the handcuffs for this one. It is Sheila Bunachellie, AKA Krutznuckle. She has a rap sheet longer than Santa's naughty list."

Harold and Rose were sitting on his bed. His arm was around her protectively, his grey Fedora securely on his head.

Pete handcuffed Sheila and sat her in Harold's recliner while he and his partner, with the help of an aide, lifted Harold's bookcase upright off the curtain, and then moved to Samuel's side of the room to lift the massive armoire off of the elderly man. Samuel was obviously in agony from his broken leg.

That's when they saw Neil. The television had crushed the back of his head, and the armoire had finished him off, sort of like when he stomped on the black widow. Karma is a killer.

The officer with Pete called to him. "We need the Coroner for this guy at the end of the bed and an ambulance for the old gent. He has a broken leg for sure, and maybe other injuries."

There was no more curtain, no more privacy, and the room was swarming with people. Pete and Roger took Sheila away, and had Calista follow to help them complete their report.

Samuel was taken by ambulance to Baylor Hospital to have his leg set. Another ambulance came for Neil, but he was pronounced DOA at the Garland General.

CHAPTER 35

The Dr. Pepper and fruitcake seemed a bit anticlimactic to Laurel, who arrived as Samuel was wheeled to the ambulance on a gurney by two stalwart EMT's.

When the elevator opened on Windom Hall, the excitement had not diminished. Aides tried to get guests to bed, but of course men were coming out into the hall to view the excitement.

Nurse Bernice was sitting at her desk, shaking after her ordeal. Rose couldn't tell if it was due to the gun, or the threat of exposure.

Laurel hurried to Harold's room. The curtain was gone, books were scattered over the floor, and the massive armoire was pushed to the back of the room again. There was a large blood stain on the foot of Samuel's bed, and a pool of blood on the floor.

Laurel gasped. "What happened here?"

Rose told the story of Neil and Sheila's attempted murder of Samuel Prescott. She and Harold had heard them talking and Rose figured out Samuel was in danger and left to get help.

"How did you have presence of mind to push over the bookcase?"

"I didn't. Harold did," Rose said proudly, looking at her beloved. He just smiled back.

Nurse Bernice had found the syringe on the floor by the foot of the bed. She put it in a baggy for evidence at the urging of Rose, who explained that Laurel and Harting, the Snoop Sisters, were in contact with the Markowitz brothers and it would go better for her if she was on their side in the investigation. Nurse Bernice had agreed with alacrity, and gave it to Calista.

"I guess we know now if Calista was a good guy or a bad guy. Apparently we were on the same quest, cleaning up Meadowdale," Laurel said.

As Charles and Darlene came in and looked at the chaos, Rose explained again what had happened.

"Those two weren't on my radar," Charles said. "Murder, who would have guessed it?"

"I'm just sorry Olive had to miss all the excitement. She would have loved to be in the big middle of this," Darlene exclaimed. "But hey, the Markowitz brothers are sending someone out here to take our deposition. Calista caught me on her way to the police station and gave me a head's up."

"Really?" Laurel asked. "We can finally turn all our evidence over to someone who can do something about Patel and Khan? And, what about the druggist?"

Rose said, "Oh, they are onto him too. Apparently Nurse Bernice was aware of the larceny and didn't do anything to stop it. If she helps identify some bigger fish they may let her slide."

Rose didn't bother going back to the duplex that night. It was very late, and with all the excitement, she knew

Ann Cornelius

she couldn't sleep. Anyway, in the morning it would be Christmas!

Nurse Betty stopped in to observe the "crime scene."

"You know, Rose, Mr. Prescott won't be coming back to this room again. I think they will either get him into an actual private room on this floor, or send him up to LaRonda. I'll have Gina clean up the bed and bring in some clean pillows and blankets. You can just bed down there for the night, if it doesn't creep you out too much."

The cops declined running yellow crime scene tape around the bed with Harold on the other side of the room.

Rose smiled. "I'd like that, Betty. You have all been so kind to us. And I am too tired to drive on home."

"Well, now that Walter has passed, Olive will be moving out. It has been such a help to have a woman on Windom who can play games, keep up with the more mobile men, and let us know if there is a problem. Kind of like unpaid labor, in a way." Nurse Betty contemplated Rose.

"On Haliburton, they have aides that do crafts and activities with the men who are fairly alert. The guests in private rooms pay more, but they get more too. It doesn't seem fair, but I'm not in charge of that. It's just, Olive made us feel we had something special too. It would be great if you could be here with Harold the way Olive was with Walter."

"I wish!" Rose said, frankly mulling over the idea. "We just can't afford it, but if we could…" she let her thought trail off.

For the first time in weeks, Rose slept peacefully through the night. Subconsciously she could feel the presence of her Harold, and she was content.

Being in Samuel's bed didn't bother her. It was better

than sleeping alone miles from her husband. And the aides had made her feel welcome.

Charles also slept well. His Christmas gifts had hit the mark on each of the special people in his life. He had just one more to deliver. He hoped it would be just what Olive needed, now that Walter was gone. No matter, it was what HE needed too.

It was nearly eleven when Darlene came in from her final smoke and settled down with soft jazz and a gin and tonic. First Laurel, now Olive. Her world was getting smaller. Life with Richard had been an adventure, but men just didn't last long enough. Charles was younger, in his late sixties, she surmised. He was someone to talk to, but it wasn't the same as women friends.

It was hard to find women who were not jealous or judgmental. Women who treated you as if you were just as smart as they were, even when you were kidding around or being a big flirt, or just being bitchy. Olive, Laurel and Rose made life bearable at Meadowdale.

Darlene finished her drink, slipped into a slinky red gown and crawled between the 800 count Egyptian cotton sheets and drifted to dream land.

The quiet, dark apartment had never given Laurel a feeling of home. She had given up so much when she moved Martin into Meadowdale. The expense was one thing, but not having a reason to come home was another. It was a cold and lonely life when you became a widow.

"Boo hoo," Laurel said to herself. "I'm just not going to have a pity party. Olive is facing the same thing, and I don't see her sniveling around."

Sighing, she got up and turned on her computer. Time to review the finances.

For ten thousand dollars she could live rent free, with just utilities each month. If she got a job and was careful with her money she would be fine. At sixty-four, it would be awhile before she filed for Social Security, if the laws didn't change. God willing and the Creeks don't rise. (That old saw, referring to President Jackson and the Creek Indian wars, was so appropriate as she faced so many changes ahead.)

Her life was at a crossroads. If she stayed in Garland, she would have a job, and some special friends. Well, for awhile anyway. The Memory Care Unit didn't keep it's "guests" very long, and then all she could count on was a lunch or two, and Bingo for excitement.

But, if she took the unknown quantity, and went to the Alhambra with her son Derreck, who knew what was waiting?

Hollywood, it even sounded like an adventure. She poured her own Dr. Pepper from a bottle into a champagne glass to celebrate.

Laurel Baley, living in Hollywood, with a son who ran a Sushi bar. It even sounded a bit glamorous. Of course, Jewel would be consulted. But, she lived so far away.

She had only visited twice since she had the two children. Jewel's husband could be a bit controlling. Their family had joined a Pentecostal church, with strict rules about watching television and appropriate entertainment. When Greg found out that Martin had done the publishing on j.j.cale's "Cocaine," he blew a gasket. Laurel hadn't dared to tell them that the gay community loved Cher's "Half

Breed," which Martin had also managed for Sal, his boss. They never came back to the Dallas area after that.

She would miss Darlene and Richard, Rose and Harold, and Olive and ....Charles? How did that make a pair, she mused.

With that, she drained her glass and went to bed. Tomorrow was Christmas.

CHAPTER 36

Christmas day dawned at a balmy forty-two degrees. Breakfast in the main dining hall was sparsely attended, so Darlene and Charles took warm sweet rolls and coffee upstairs to Windom Hall to see how Rose was doing.

Rose was helping Harold get ready for breakfast. He had already had his tea and newspaper (the San Francisco Free Press was his favorite), and was donning the black wool driving cap.

"Guess we are the new team, with Laurel and Harting, the Snoop Sisters gone." Darlene said brightly. "What will we call ourselves?"

"Unemployed," Charles said, a bit grumpily.

They all laughed at that.

"Not quite yet," Nurse Yvonne said from the doorway. "You still need to do depositions for the police on the two killers, and whatever else it was you uncovered."

"Also, just got word that Fredrick Stone, the Markowitz brothers' attorney is coming in on Thursday to talk to you all about the tape, the video, and something else. I didn't get it all. Nurse Bernice filled me in over the phone. I guess you guys are heroes."

"Then we need to get Laurel here, and let Olive know," suggested Charles.

Dr. Singh looked into the room.

"I understand Walter will be cremated, and they are having a simple service on Wednesday down in Elgin. I am sorry none of us will be part of it. However, I was able to secure a room for Mrs. Harting in Independent Living."

Darlene asked him sharply, "And how do you know all this?"

Dr. Singh came further into the room to explain. "Mrs. Harting called to thank me for my help with Walter, and inquired if I could facilitate a move within the three day period, since she would be busy with funeral arrangements. I was happy to help."

"Well, I'll be," was all Charles could say, a big smile on his face.

Darlene was happy too. "Guess the old gang hasn't broken up after all."

"If Laurel leaves, you could be the new Snoop Sister," Charles suggested.

"Don't leave me out," Rose protested. "There could be three Snoop Sisters." They nodded their agreement. "The three Mouseketeers it is!" proclaimed Darlene. "After all, one of the original Mouseketeers was named Darlene."

They laughed at that, turning their attention to coffee and cookies. Since so many visitors brought sweets for the guests, and most of those guests had medical problems that kept them from having too many sweets, the nurse quickly passed them on to other visitors.

Around ten o'clock Darlene called Laurel.

"Come on over for lunch. We are sending out for pizza

and having a party. We are all giving gifts to Charles, so bring a white elephant."

"You got it!" Laurel said. It was early, but she called Derreck anyway.

"Merry Christmas," she said. "Now, tell me about this place in Hollywood."

Derreck filled her in on what he knew.

The Alhambra was an older building in an area of Hollywood. It was a small, two story office building which had seen many changes in the last forty years. But, it had good occupants, and his partner, Kenji Takada, was using it as an investment.

The three hundred thousand Derreck put up from his condo sale was for the renovation on the Sushi Bar, which he would run as the main chef.

Derreck's apartment was behind the kitchen area, and Laurel's would be on the second floor. Three of the businesses were open weekdays, and three, along with the Sushi Bar, were open on Saturday as well. Nothing operated Sunday.

"The Alhambra was owned by a Syrian or Iranian man who needed the money quick to leave the country," Derreck said. "So it was a steal. You will love the charm of it. And, get this, Court Courier, a legal court filing service has a position for you if you want it!"

"Sounds very, uh, continental, a whole new world view," Laurel said thoughtfully. "I can handle that. Can I use my Spanish?"

"Yeah, there is a Mexican lawyer in a downstairs office, and a Guatemalan Factor, a guy who works with clothing designers, upstairs. A Chinese herbal doctor is there too. It's a real melting pot, Mom."

She laughed. "Give me two weeks so I can give notice and I'll head out."

When Laurel arrived on Windom Hall, the aides moved Samuel's chair next to the Harold's recliner and added two chairs from the dining area. There was much conversation and laughter before Darlene declared it was Christmas gift time.

"I already gave all mine out, except for Olive's," said Charles with a curious look on his face.

"That's right," Darlene said, nodding in agreement. "Now it is our turn to gift YOU."

Rose gave him a small bag which contained the beautiful blue and green muffler she had been knitting.

Charles smile, "Thank you Rose, and Harold."

Darlene handed him a small box which held a silver money clip adorned with a 1954 Silver Dollar. "Richard doesn't need it anymore, and I think you'll look spiffy spending some of that dough you have in your new life."

Charles protested. "I really don't have a new life."

"My gift to you," said Laurel. "I talked with an attorney at my office. He said Judge Fraxtion could do a competency hearing and get you back to the land of the living. Then, if you want your sister to be your Executor when you need one later, that can be arranged. Dr. Singh said he would vouch for you, as did Calista, believe it or not."

"And that means…?" Charles was speechless.

"That means you really can live independently, here or anywhere. You will be able to be a consenting adult again," Darlene exclaimed. Charles just sat there, his mind spinning.

It felt like Grand Central Station. Nurse Bernice was on

vacation, but the substitute stopped in to see what was going on, and to get the scoop on last night's activities. Several other visitors were also curious about the police presence the night before, so the story was told again and again about Neil and Sheila and the foiled attempts on Uncle Samuel's life.

The pizza man delivered six pizza's, as instructed. Two were pepperoni, one with mushroom (for Laurel and Darlene), one meat lover's (for the men), one cheese only, (for Charles and Richard) and one with pineapple and Canadian bacon for Rose.

Carolers from Assisted Living came over and they all stood in the visitor's dining area and sang Rudolph, Jingle Bells, and of course, Silent Night. It was a Merry Christmas after all.

CHAPTER 37

Thursday things got back to normal, as normal as they could be. The regulars were back on staff. Olive was back at Meadowdale, although it was downstairs in Indie, not on Windom Hall.

Her son, Gordon, had supervised the move Tuesday while Olive was in Elgin preparing for Walter's service. She had a new bed and dresser, a nice desk for her laptop, and rolling chair, two bookcases, and a kitchen table and two chairs. The two old brown recliners sat in front of the entertainment center as it had in their shared room, in case Olive had a visitor.

Like Charles, her mini kitchenette had a tiny refrigerator, microwave and counter with a small sink and one cupboard. Independent seniors like to have a bowl of cereal or soup, a carton of milk and a loaf of bread on hand. It wasn't always convenient to go to the dining hall if a favorite show was on or there was a nap to be taken.

As Olive was organizing her books, there was a knock at her door and Myrtle breezed in.

"Welcome to the neighborhood! Darlene has told us all about you and Walter. I am really sorry he is gone. That is tough," Myrtle held out a shiny pink bag with a silver bow. "Welcome."

Olive took the bag and opened it as Myrtle sat down in one of the recliner. "Don't mind if I do," she said with a grin.

"Oh, yes, please sit down," Olive said, a bit flustered. "What is all this?"

"It is our welcome wagon for Indie living on the ladie's side. You get our newsletter, with all the skinny on coming events, birthdays and stuff. There is also a Meadowdale official fan, and most important, the wristband for you room key."

Olive took it out and looked at it, her brow furrowed. "I have a key ring."

Myrtle huffed and heaved herself from the recliner. She took the rubber wrist band from Olive. "Where is your key?"

Olive retrieved it from the hook on the kitchen wall. Myrtle took it from the key ring and attached it to the wrist band.

"Look Olive, there have been lots of thefts around here. Not that it looks like you have much to steal (Olive gave her a sharp look at this), but you can't be too careful." Myrtle handed her the wrist band.

"We all lock our doors now when we go anywhere. Now you are one of the girls in the Go-Go Gang." Myrtle grinned and pushed her glasses back up on her nose.

"You can either walk down the long corridor and out to the dining room, or join us in riding the golf cart shuttle. There are movies at Assisted Living on Fridays, and Bingo and, oh, just lots of stuff to do. You won't have time to be sad or lonely."

Olive gave her a long look. "I think I need time to adjust. My husband just passed away, and this is new to me."

About then Darlene breezed in, took one look at a stone faced Olive and Myrtle glaring at her with a defensive attitude.

"I was just being friendly," Myrtle said huffily.

"And I am sure Olive appreciates it, don't you kiddo?" Darlene said affectionately, putting an arm around Olives shoulder.

Olive relaxed a bit, and grudgingly said, "Thank you for the welcome wagon. I am sure that in time this will be something I will appreciate." Her eyes glistened with tears.

Myrtle looked strickened. "I am sorry. I guess it was too soon. Sorry Olive, Darlene. I've got to run." She pushed her glasses back on her nose and headed for the door.

"Geeze Olive, I guess you got ambushed. Myrtle means well. She can be a swell friend, just give her some time." Darlene said sympathetically.

"I just came to tell you the Markowitz brother's lawyer is coming tomorrow to talk to us about the situation, whatever that means. Are you okay?"

Olive nodded and hugged Darlene.

"Just give me some time alone to process. I know I will need new friends. Right now I appreciate the ones I have, like you, Darlene." Olive gave her a sad smile and walked her to the door. She thought a minute, then turned the lock.

CHAPTER 38

A flinty lawyer from Houston, Frederick Stone, arrived to talk with each of them individually and take their deposition. He had a horse-faced paralegal with him who had one of those steno boxes like they use at trials, and no matter how fast they talked, she was able to keep up. Darlene tried to jabber, but the paralegal only asked her to repeat one time, when she said, "Crimenently, I mean, Jesus-H-Christ! Khan is pulling a fast one!"

After they had given their testimony, Calista met with them to explain what was going on.

"You see, when Medicare and Medicaid got involved due to the creative billing of Dr. Patel, it meant an audit of all three facilities. Saul and Abe Markowitz are businessmen. If there was a scandal, it could hurt Pineview in Houston and Shadow Mountain in Austin as well as Meadowdale Manor."

"The Corporation has invested in a Pill Box Pharmacy and Load and Lock Storage Unit in all three cities as well. That's all. The three are symbiotic, meaning they help one another. The pharmacist at the Pill Box fills all the prescriptions for the facility, so they are guaranteed good price and quality of medication, and when a guest leaves and doesn't want the furnishings, the people at the storage unit get a flat rate to remove it all."

"Now, some stuff can go to a charity, and the Corporation gets a write-off. If it is better quality, the furniture is auctioned in a storage locker, like for past due rent. The amount of rent goes to the Corporation, and anything above that goes to the operators of the storage facility. Everyone is happy, and there is no problem."

The group had reviewed what they knew and shared it with Calista and the attorney.

In this case, the Snoop Sisters discovered Amy was stealing drugs and selling them to Vincent Rupert, the Pharmacist, who was repackaging them and selling them back to Meadowdale. Highly unethical to say the least. But, she wasn't the only one.

Calista agreed. "Nurse Racket and DeShawn on LaRhonda were also doing it. Poor Racket, she thought Vincent Rupert had a thing for her, but it was only the access to better narcotics."

"So Load and Lock was legit?" Darlene asked.

"Absolutely. The real problem was with the theft of other items and selling them at Stellar Auction. That was Dr. Patel and DeShawn's little scheme," Calista shared.

"How did that work?" Laurel wanted to know.

"DeShawn was an opportunist, and just rifled through drawers on LaRonda and Windom Hall to find things to sell for drug money."

"When Dr. Patel found out, he knew he had something on DeShawn and could use him to his advantage."

"Dr. Patel began to spend more time on the first floor, where he had a legitimate reason to be. His little old ladies welcomed him gladly. If he saw something of value that might not be missed, he passed that information on to DeShawn."

"Since DeShawn worked nights, he could clock out, wait in the employee lounge until the breakfast crowd gathered and sneak in to get the goodies. The auction house had no way of knowing they were working as a fence."

"DeShawn did it for the drug money, but Dr. Patel needed money to pay off Khan. It doesn't matter why they did it, the guests here were getting robbed. It had to stop," Calista said.

Charles looked at her with concern. "When you hear the recording, you can tell he really didn't *want* to act deceptively. Khan forced him to somehow. I just wonder what he had on Patel."

Calista looked sympathetic. "Patel's record was fine until he came here. When Mr. Presley left two years ago to run Southgate Hospital, Patel recommended Fawad Khan to replace him."

"They had met at med school. Khan finished his pre-med at the bottom of his class, so he went on to major in business and worked mainly with small hospitals."

"I'm sure Patel didn't know Khan was a rat in Brooks Brothers clothing."

Charles agreed. "I overheard Khan laughing about Patel's situation to his secretary Dalia. Khan said Hardik and his wife Deepika had an arranged wedding when they were very young. Her parents put Patel through medical school so he would support them in their old age."

"They also demanded a grandson. It took four tries before they got the boy, Salman. The kid was really scrawny.

That gave Khan a chuckle. I almost crawled over the bird cage to hear all of this."

"Apparently Deepika has never liked Hardik, so she spends much of her time back in the state of Gujarat in India with her parents and her children," Calista said. "No one around here knew what was going on with Dr. Patel. He always did his work and didn't say much. I mean, who notices if the doctor's wife is around or not?"

"So what was the blackmail?" asked Laurel.

"Well, apparently Dr. Patel has gotten some affection from an aide or two over the past three years. Not sex, just a little slap and tickle. But when one of them went to Khan to complain, he did a report. He threatened to submit it if Hardik did not do exactly as he requested." Charles said angrily.

"How did you find that out?" asked Darlene.

"When I went through his files, you know, when he left for the WinStar and his secretary Dalia went to get her nails done. There it was, the report in a file marked IMPORTANT, and a note that Patel had signed saying he was aware that if he did not do as instructed, the file would be released," Charles said grimly.

"Yikes!" exclaimed Darlene. "That is so evil. Dr. Patel really didn't get anything out of the relationship with Khan, did he? He not only had to pay blackmail, but do things that went against his conscious."

"Well, the Auditors aren't impressed with his good intentions. He will lose his medical license for at least four years," Calista said with finality.

"And his wife and kids," asked Rose softly. "This has to be hard on them."

Calista looked at her sympathetically. "In his culture, the smartest child is chosen to get the best education, and in return support the entire family. Patel was the chosen one. His wife will stand by him, even if she won't live with him."

"If he can't be a doctor, what will he do?" Rose persisted.

"Administration," Calista admitted with a shrug.

"Abe Markowitz knows Dr. Patel is a good doctor, so they offered him a transfer to a small hospital in Minnesota. Their Administrator died in a crash a week ago and they are desperate. Dr. Patel's background and knowledge is a good fit. He will lose his license to practice, but he still has leadership potential, so it may work out."

Olive spoke up. "Rani told me she is moving up to night shift on LaRonda. What is that about?"

Laurel said, "Dr. Singh let me know about her promotion too. It sounds good."

Calista sat back and looked at the ladies.

"Okay, here's the skinny. Rani gets her four year nursing degree in May. That means she is nearly the kind of RN that can be hired as a charge nurse. Racket is gone, and we have a long term temp in place to hold that position until Rani graduates. In the meantime, she will be up there learning the ropes, getting ready to take charge. With this new position, it is rumored that she and Dr. Singh will be making it legal. He asked her to marry him at Christmas, before all the excitement. She said yes."

"Is Dr. Singh taking Dr. Patel's place?" asked Laurel.

Olive looked at her sharply and explained, "He is just a P.A., a physician's assistant, not a physician."

"That's right," agreed Calista. "Dr. Punjab has agreed

to take over that task, as long as Dr. Singh will continue to do the day-to-day medical work."

"What about the Medicare fraud," asked Charles. "Will they close us down?"

Calista smiled at that. "No, that is why Fredrick Stone gets the big bucks. The Corporation will pay a hefty fine and prove it was just this facility, just Dr. Patel. He loses his license, the government gets their money, and everyone is happy."

"Not everyone," fumed Charles. "That Fawad Khan should pay for his part is all of this."

"Have you seen him recently?" asked Calista.

"No, I guess he hasn't come back from WinStar yet," Charles muttered.

"Oh, he came back alright," Calista said. "And, he DID win this time, about fifteen thousand dollars. The police got him when he crossed the Texas border and they confiscated all that cash."

"You see, he had been embezzling from Rest Assured, that insurance fraud they were running. That is a federal offense."

"Rest Assured has been closed down. The brothers knew nothing about it, or being on the board of Smith Funeral Home. Smith won't be doing any business with Meadowdale again either."

Laurel said sharply, "Well, they would not cremate Martin until they had three on ice, they said. Now THAT has to be illegal."

"Actually" Calista corrected her, "that isn't illegal. They save money on fuel to only heat the ovens once. It was the Rest Assured folk that got stuck. They paid full price for a private cremation and secure ashes, but who knows WHO they got in their little urn?"

"Rest Assured is closed? I have my final wishes with them!" exclaimed Charles.

"No problem. All clients will be fully refunded and directed to a new end of life advisor. Their charter got pulled, and all those royalties they siphoned off are in a big tangle. Judge Cheatem will probably be thrown off the bench as well, unless he slinks quietly away. Now THAT is the real scandal," Calista smugly declared.

"So who is the new administrator?" Rose asked impatiently.

"A former nun, Herldine Gnomer, arrives this weekend. She comes highly recommended and seems caring and competent," Calista said smugly

"A nun?" protested Rose. "Will she be able to handle Meadowdale?"

Calista laughed. "She handled St. Bernadine's High School, and Montview Terrace. This place will be a cinch for Miss Gnomer. I think she will be replacing the birds with guinea pigs."

Darlene explained to Calista, "We wondered if you were a good guy or bad guy."

"Oh I'm one of the good ones," said Calista proudly. "And now that you Snoop Sisters and company have cleared up the mess here, I'm heading back to run my company, Temporary Medical Personnel and Billing Company, here in Dallas. This was just a temp job for me too."

She hugged each of them before she left. They were glad she had been one of the good guys.

CHAPTER 39

"Okay," said Darlene, "what was the gift you had for Olive? She wouldn't tell us."

Charles blushed, and smoothed down his worsted wool jacket. He obviously was uncomfortable discussing it as he cleared his throat twice.

"It was a cruise up the Danube to see all the castles. I have tickets for the same cruise, but because of my situation, I was afraid to try and travel. Once I get cleared, I guess we can both go. It will be a real adventure."

Olive smiled. "I've always wanted to go up the Danube. He also gave me a big book on the castles so I can read up on them. We plan on going this fall, don't we Charles?"

He blushed again.

"So I guess you found that someone who is warm, compassionate, intelligent, a bit feisty and full of vigor after all," laughed Laurel. "I thought you were trying to make a pass at me!"

"Hell, I was nervous when you gave me those fabulous heels!" exclaimed Darlene.

"Well, I guess I could take this as making a pass," said Olive, "but I am going to see it as two friends with a lot in common who both like to travel, to talk, and to enjoy what is left of life."

Nurse Bernice came in and motioned to Rose. "Phone call, dear," she said.

The group soon forgot about Rose as they chatted about everything Calista had revealed.

When she came back into the room, Rose was crying.

"What's wrong," Darlene asked, hugging her.

"Not wrong, just so….right!" Rose said, sniffling and wiping her eyes.

"Huh?"

"Well, that call was from Mr. Stone, the attorney. It seems, upon the recommendation from the staff here, I have been offered a room with Harold for as long as he lives. I still have to pay for his care, but mine is free, since I will actually be a caregiver." Rose stopped to catch her breath.

"There was a reward for Sheila, and it goes to Harold and me. It is only ten thousand dollars, but that helps, especially since I won't have other expenses if I move in here. They want me to take your place, Olive. To be the ray of sunshine, as they put it."

Olive hugged her. "I'll be right downstairs with Darlene and Charles. And, we will all be coming up to see you and Harold, and of course, Richard. You aren't alone. We won't abandon you."

"Not like Laurel is," grumped Charles.

"Now, now," Olive said. "She is still here for a week or so, and we still have a few loose ends to clear up with the police."

On Friday, they all trooped down to the police station where Pete interviewed them. The stenographer took them one at a time and when it was done, Pete and his superior took them into a larger room to catch them up on what had actually occurred.

"Awhile back, we were alerted by WinStar that Fawad Khan was dropping heavy money, and at one point had used a company credit card to finance his gambling habit. It was just a courtesy call. Anyway, we contacted the Markowitz brothers, and they agreed to let us put a mole, Calista, into the facility to see if anything else was going on."

"Then the auditors caught the billing problems of Dr. Patel. There seemed to be a pattern. Next, Calista uncovered some medical malfeasance with the death certificates and the problems with Rest Assured. But, we didn't have all the proof we needed."

"Since that time, we discovered that Smith's wife and Judge Dewey Cheatem are cousins. That Smith family was becoming heir to every music, oil and other royalty possible where no living relative could be found. The Court clerk was also involved. Again, the Snoop Sisters gave us the lead we needed." Pete nodded to them in acknowledgement.

"At the time we were unaware of Amy Armstrong and Vincent Rupert at the Pill Box and their theft and resale of drugs. Laurel's video helped us out there. And then, the taped conversation which Charles obtained tied the pieces together. We had our case against Rupert, Armstrong, Patel and Khan."

"You Snoop Sisters even helped with DeShawn Brown and the thefts. Stellar Auction got quite a shock on that one." Pete gave a satisfied smile.

Then he said earnestly, "But this thing with Neil Armstrong came out of left field."

"When Corine and Carlene pulled a fast one with the private room act, it saved Prescott's life. In a private room, one of those Plan B's that Sheila had used effectively in her prior relationships would have done him in."

"Marrying old, wealthy men and then knocking them off was her M.O. Two times it was antifreeze, once it was those herbal brownies with a strychnine cocktail, and one time it was too much Viagra. Anyway, she picked the wrong old man, and the wrong yuppy schnook."

"Neil Armstrong wasn't a monster. He was just a greedy, inept millenial without a conscious or the skills to complete a given task. That's why he lost job after job. He had the credentials and the looks to get the jobs, but no follow through."

"That is probably another reason he is dead and Uncle Samuel is alive."

"First, he flubbed the antifreeze milkshake. The old man was a diabetic. Calista had the presence of mind to gather the evidence and give it to us to check out. At that point he was on our radar."

"I have to give it to him for creativity. That little Plexiglas box held a black widow. Thanks to Olive, we were able to trace it to Pete's Precious Poison Pets. Who knows how that went wrong. It may be hiding in the armoire that crushed Armstrong."

"The third Plan B, or maybe the fourth, was Sheila again, with the brownies laced with marijuana. That resulted in the firing of two employees on the third floor. Prescott never got a chance to eat the brownies."

"So, the final Plan B, according to Sheila, was to inject Prescott with her little cocktail and just let him die a painful death, in the hopes that Patel would write it off as a heart attack."

"The worst part is the terrible twins, Corine and Carlene, demanded we certify Neil as a murderer so they could get his portion of the estate. I mean, he's dead, so he couldn't inherit anyway."

"Turns out in the trust, Neil's death means his portion is not divided with the surviving heirs, but goes to Northeast Missouri State University for the study of giant newt chromosomes. Apparently the giant newt, like the blind newt, has some amazing DNA that may change medical science."

"I guess that clears it up," sighed Laurel and squeezed Olive's hand.

"Rose and Harold will get the reward for the arrest and conviction of Sheila Krutznuckle. One of the families whose father she killed offered the reward, and if it weren't for Harold's quick actions, and Rose getting help, Prescott would have been killed and Sheila would have escaped," Pete said proudly.

"What about Uncle Samuel?" asked Rose, sympathetically. "Everyone forgets about him."

"He's got a private room on Haliburton when he gets out of rehab at Baylor. Turns out his wasn't a memory failure, as his relatives assumed. He is just a weird old scientific genius. No one can understand a word he says but another brilliant scientist, like those in the giant newt study. But, he said he would like to be near Rose and Harold. So there you are," said Pete.

"So the bottom line," Peter admitted, "is that Laurel

and Harting, the Snoop Sisters, got us all out of another fine mess, as the real Laurel and Hardy would say."

The Meadowdale Gang left the police station in the facility van, laughing all the way.

"What shall we call this caper?" Charles asked.

"The case of the Black Widow and the Astro-nut," suggested Darlene.

"The Snoop Sisters and Company shut down Medical Malpractice," suggested Laurel.

"The Last Ride of the Snoop Sisters, and the formation of the Meadowdale Gang," said Olive.

"Now that you are moving, Laurel, it won't be the same. However, I think the four of us, Rose and Darlene, Charles and I, will be on the alert for any sneaky wrong doing here. That was what we were trying to do, protect seniors in nursing homes and retirement villages."

"We'll hold their feet to the fire," agreed Charles. "If that Miss Gnomer doesn't do right by our residents, we will let the brothers know immediately."

"And Dr. Punjab better not be moving guests to make more money for the Corporation," Rose said firmly.

Laurel smiled. "You guys have got this. You don't need me, but if you do, just whistle."

At that, she threw her long brown hair back from her eyes like Lauren Bacall and grinned.

She was ready for new adventures in La La Land. The Meadowdale Gang could handle Garland, Texas pretty well.

Printed in the United States
By Bookmasters